NEW EARTH: ARC

Devon C Ford

PRESS

Published by Vulpine Press in the United Kingdom in 2018

Cover by Claire Wood

ISBN: 978-1-910780-98-5

www.vulpine-press.com

Dedicated to H who fought hard to win the world record in worst sickness during pregnancy and excused everything with the claim of 'growing a human.'

Author's Note

I recently read a review which slated a good friend's book as being "a total work of fiction."

It was a fiction book, a totally constructed story that, whilst based on real science and potential events, was in its essence just a story.

This is what writers do; we make stuff up and people can choose to read it. Sometimes it's good, and sometimes it isn't, but it does exactly what it claims to do: it tells a story.

I say this at the beginning of this book by way of an apology. I'm no rocket scientist, and I'm no geneticist, but I am a story teller. So please, if my calculations of Earth's orbital patterns aren't quite up to astro-physicist levels, or maybe (no spoilers) I've created in my mind something that couldn't actually exist within the laws of science that we know, then I ask that you let it go…

It reminds me once of an argument I had whilst watching a film about dinosaurs being brought back to life. The argument was about the type of weapon used not correlating to the bullet hole in the glass it left and raged for quite some time until we were both brought up on it. The question was simply put: "Why are you two arguing about guns, but not the fact that dinosaurs are there?"

That shut me up.

So please, read the story, and take it for what it is.

;)

Prologue

Deep Earth Orbit
January 19, 2033

I took my last look at Earth through the window, or hopefully Earth as I knew it anyway, feeling almost numb for the knowledge of what was going to happen.

"Annie?" I said aloud, hearing the soft, muted tone of acknowledgement hum from the speakers in each section to signify that my creation was listening. "Exact time until impact?"

Her synthesized voice filled the small, round corridor I was floating in. "Time until impact is nineteen hours, thirty-seven minutes and eight seconds, with a variant threshold of forty-nine seconds. Recommend you begin cryoprocedures within six hours, Dr. Anderson."

"Thank you, may as well do it now," I said absently, treating Annie politely as I always did, like she was a person who was concerned for my feelings instead of what she truly was: an integrated computer interface operating system usefully informing me of a forty-nine second margin for error.

Placing a hand on the glass and almost covering the little blue and green orb I was born, raised, and lived on, I said my final goodbyes in silence. I turned to propel my body horizontally toward the access to the upper corridor of the ARC, or *Ark* as we'd quickly decided to pronounce it all those years ago, when it was still the International Space Station. I'd been on board for eighteen months, and although fully acclimated to the environment, I doubted I would ever really get used to it.

I'd intentionally taken a specific route to get my last view of the planet we were all born on. The return route to my assigned cryopod took me past almost everyone else aboard, which was just about everyone as the only remaining people awake were the two maintenance specialists who would be reminded to rotate every twelve months by Annie. They would go into cryo for six months to cover the impact and the aftermath, then Annie would wake them to take their turns as the custodians of humanity.

Rank after rank of white tubes looking like torpedoes lined the chambers, all of which could be individually sealed in the event of anything catastrophic happening, and the ARC as a whole could be preserved with minimal losses. All of that was controlled by Annie, following her in-depth internal flowcharts of decision making which had taken me close to fifteen years to develop. The new subroutines for her to follow and enact accounted for almost a decade of that, when she was repurposed to be the caretaker of the human race.

On arriving at my assigned pod, I spun myself around lazily, allowing the zero gravity to do most of the work, and settled myself in to the soft straps.

"I'm ready, Annie," I said out loud as the pod began to flash a sequence of lights denoting the cryotube was starting up, then placed the breathing mask over my face and needlessly adjusted the tracker device on my left wrist. I saw no sense in waiting or delaying it, as it wasn't as though I could stay up late to watch the big show.

"Commencing cryosleep now," came Annie's soothing tones, making me feel grateful for the year and a half I'd spent working on finding the right voice for her program. "Goodnight, David. Sleep well."

With that, I closed my eyes and breathed in the subtle combination of gasses that would put me under before my body was frozen into a state of hibernation.

So long, Earth, I thought to myself, *see you in a hundred years.*

Part 1:

Pre-Event Earth

Chapter 1

Mumbai

May 25, 2021

As international billionaire entrepreneurs went, Amir Weatherby was young when he rose to the head of the family business. Their portfolio was so diverse that not one single person in the organization knew what fingers were in what pies, and there was a chief executive for each continent, often ones for individual countries depending on the concentration of assets and investments. The company, Icarus Investments, was so vast that it was everywhere and nowhere. They paid taxes to no country, and any organization that went after them for revenue ended up losing.

Amir, educated at all the right establishments and spending his time between his mother's family in her native India and his father's multiple estates in the US, was the epitome of the entitled elite. He appeared as a rich Saudi oil prince, spoke like he grew up on the upper east side of Manhattan, but was equally at home walking the sweltering, packed streets of the Indian capital.

Nothing was beyond his grasp; everything had a price that he could easily afford, and he always got what he wanted. Despite that privileged elitism, he was a likeable, charismatic young man.

The company was responsible for the first self-driving cars, for the automated drone delivery systems active in some major cities, for technological breakthroughs in ballistic body armor, as well as the armor-piercing munitions capable of defeating it. They sold indiscriminately to the entire world, albeit through a series of blind companies so no direct scandal could ever taint the company name.

When he turned twenty-four, he used his newly gained law degree to advise the best team of lawyers in the Netherlands in a case that was watched eagerly all over the world. The government was suing Icarus for millions in taxes for parts of the assets operating in their territory, and a win would reverberate over the globe and set a precedent for everyone to follow suit.

Amir's father, Paul Weatherby, had taken steps to negate any losses and moved all of their European assets into a dozen other companies which would take years to follow, but Amir was confident of winning the case in court.

When they did win, the counter-suit he levelled at the federally collective twelve provinces of the Netherlands threatened to bankrupt the country. If not for the intervention of the European Union and a number of behind-closed-doors concessions made to company limitations, then they would have been finished.

Two years later, after losing Weatherby Senior to a sudden and unexpected heart attack, Amir calmly put on a ten-thousand-dollar suit and gave a heartfelt press release to the world on the sad passing of a great man. A visionary. Within six months, Amir had reassigned the majority of assets into research and development with an undisguised view toward commercial space travel. The privatization of government assets was an ongoing trend throughout the entire west, whereas the Russian and Chinese continents were becoming increasingly insular. Amir had acquired entire launch stations in former Soviet Union countries, had doubled the wages and conditions of anyone working at NASA or their sister organization of the Jet Propulsion Laboratory, or JPL, and invested so heavily in the Indian Space Research Organization, or ISRO, that he found himself in the unique position of being able to influence the country's policy priorities if not directly dictate their mandates. He even managed to privatize the running of the ISS, International Space Station, after the Chinese and Russians withdrew their personnel and funding from the program, leaving a financial vacuum which begged to be filled.

One of his biggest gambles was the acquisition of the Hubble telescope program, which was suffering with the reduction in investment from all the space-capable nations. This gamble ultimately paid off as, when it was being repositioned for full-time Mars reconnaissance, the operators saw the asteroid.

2021QX84 was what they had called it and Amir thought that was stupid. The report came with a warning that the trajectory of the asteroid would take it past Earth, at least inside the solar system, but nothing more accurate could be said at that time. He knew that dozens of such warnings came each year, and each year world-devastating hunks of rock and mineral and ice passed through their solar system without causing the panic that such knowledge would inevitably bring.

Leaning back in his chair and frowning at the screen bearing the ambiguous report, he picked up his cell phone and dialed the number for the first rocket scientist he had ever met. It was picked up inside of three rings, and the person on the other end sounded sleepy.

"I'm sorry, Ian," he said as he made the lightning-fast calculations in his head to tell him that he had just called someone at a little past four in the morning, their time, "I didn't think before I dialed. I have ju—"

"I wasn't sleeping," came the voice from the other end. "I haven't left work since yesterday."

That made Amir sit up, as though he now saw the seriousness of the report that had been sat in his inbox. Ian Edwards was not a man prone to panic. Having spent much of his life working long hours for NASA at Two Independence Square in D.C. instead of at home with his wife and two sons, he had jumped at the chance for a better life in a warmer climate working for Amir. The fact that he was still at work spoke volumes.

"Is it this 2021QX thing?" Amir asked him, holding his breath for the three-second pause on the other end to pass.

"Yes," Edwards confirmed worryingly, "our supercomputers have run the simulation twice now, and are running a third. It doesn't look good," he intoned ominously.

"What kind of 'not good'?" Amir responded as he rose from his desk to pace the large office. Edwards paused on the other end of the line again.

"Ian?" Amir prompted.

"It's …" he began, sounding unsure, "it's going to hit us, we think, depending on the gravitational pull of the sun as it passes through our solar system."

Amir said nothing, letting the phone drop away from his ear slightly before Edwards' voice brought him back.

"Yes, I'm here, go on," he said.

"I was saying that it's not certain, but we could be looking at the big one. A dinosaur-killing sized event, only bigger ..." He trailed away, waiting for some answer, some child-like hope of reassurance to come from his employer and benefactor. Instead he heard the coldness of the response.

"Who else knows about this?" Amir asked.

"Me and a handful here," he said. "Three people working on the Hubble and that's it. The Hubble people sent it down to us, but they do that with four or five a month. Usually we can tell within an hour that whatever asteroid they've found will pass us safely by millions of miles away, but this one—"

"I want total lockdown," Amir interrupted him, "no media, nobody who doesn't already know can find out, and no government report."

"We have to tell the govern—" Edwards began explaining, reminding Amir of their contractual obligations when acquiring the Hubble, that every contact report had to be sent to NASA for analysis.

"Give them a different report," Amir cut in again, knowing fullwell what his obligations were, "just don't tell them that it will hit us. Don't even hint at it. Let them think it will pass by." He paused as he shot his cuff to look at the Omega on his wrist. "I'll be there in around ... seventeen hours." And with that, he ended the call and dialed another number.

"I need a jet ready for takeoff in half an hour," he ordered into the phone, "with enough fuel to get to Texas."

~

At the other end of the terminated call, Ian Edwards looked at the cell phone in his hand for a moment.

Have I just been ordered to lie to the government about an asteroid that will hit the earth? he asked himself, then considered what would happen if he didn't. He looked at the initial calculations, measuring size and speed of the space missile and accounting for variables in the trajectory, and knew with absolute certainty that this thing would wipe out Earth if it hit them. Then he looked at the impact predictions, his eyes resting on one thing and staying there.

It'll take nearly twelve years to get here, he thought, *what would we do to each other in twelve years when there are no consequences?*

Deciding against being personally responsible for worldwide anarchy, he took the report to his desk, adjusted his seat, swallowed hard, and typed out a new version to send to his former colleagues at NASA.

Chapter 2

Research Facility in Estonia
November 30, 2021

I guess I was a bit of a loner even before. I had been at the company's research facility in the Estonian countryside for a little over two years after my project had been picked up and funded by Amir Weatherby's company. My invention had been used all over the world before this, but my previous bad contract meant that nobody knew it was mine, and I didn't have access to the profits for it to be developed. I was a genius and an idiot all at once. I knew that actors and singers needed agents to stop them getting screwed over, but for a robotics geek from Massachusetts with a pair of degrees in robotic engineering and computer linguistic programming, which I earned at the same time I might add, before blasting through my doctorate, I was just a dumb kid who got played by the big corporation.

My reluctance to jump straight back in bed with another big business after I earned less than half a percent of my last invention's net worth was pretty obvious, like a recent wound. But when a guy lands a helicopter literally on your front lawn to invite you personally to work for him at a state-of-the-art facility, it kind of impresses.

So that's what I did. I packed up all my things into storage, gave notice to my landlord, and I left. The decision to leave the States was an easy one, having no family left inside of a comfortable drive and nobody around that I really spoke to anyway.

Hell, I was so wrapped up in my shoestring project that I didn't even have time for a cat.

There were other people working at the facility too, so it wasn't as though I spent my entire life only talking to Annie, or to give her proper title, Advanced Non-Sentient Intelligence Interface, or ANII for short.

Annie was an evolution of my first invention. Having a voice-controlled computer doing things like playing your music and adding detergent to your shopping list was cute and all, but I wanted more from her than the average soccer mom did. I had just finished wasting a huge amount of time on refining the right voice for her, and had been given clearance for her to be integrated into the facility's control system to help with the running and to test it for efficiency. The original plan was to hardwire speakers and microphones into every room and corridor, but someone from high up in the company arrived with a list of questions for me from Amir.

Could the ANII be programmed to operate a series of systems without human control? Sure.

Could the ANII operate for extended periods without human interaction? Sure she could, it's not like she has feelings.

Could the ANII run multiple systems and diagnostics at once, in different locations, for extended periods? Given enough memory, sure she could.

"Hey, what's all this about?" I asked the guy as he was tapping away at his phone with the answers. Jabbing his thumb at the screen of the smartphone, which was designed, manufactured, and retailed by the company, naturally, he cursed as he couldn't get the signal for the message to go out.

"You need to connect to our system down here," I told him. Seeing his look as he was about to ask for the network password I cut him off. "I got this," I told him, then tapped at my own tablet to connect to Annie. She wasn't hard-wired into the facility yet, but she was connected to the computer controls.

"Annie?" I said, then listened for the muted beep from the tablet speaker which told me she was listening. "Can you connect my friend's phone here to the network?" A two-tone beep sounded to tell me she understood the question before the speaker on the guy's cell phone came to life.

"You are now connected to the facilities network," she said to him. "Should you need it, an operating guide has been sent to your inbox."

The suit dropped his jaw and looked at me. I shrugged, even though it was impressive for anyone who hadn't seen any of her tricks before, because all it did was follow a programmed response for logical reasoning.

Annie 'knew' that by saying *my friend* I didn't mean for her to connect anything of mine to the system. She 'knew' that she then had to search for an unconnected device near to me and connect it. It was child's play for her, but the guy acted like he'd been touched by a ghost.

"It's just programming, man, relax," I told him, but he still seemed alarmed.

"Annie?" I said again, waiting for the beep and intending to put the guy's mind at ease. "Are you alive?"

The two-tone sounded again before she spoke. "No. I am a sequence of programmed algorithms which may seem like I am making sentient choices, but I am not."

The guy looked at me, a smile creeping onto his face as he was about to ask what they all asked: *Isn't that exactly what she'd say if she was alive and pretending?*

"She's just programming. Every action and the logical consequence is her following a set of rules which she isn't even aware of. She can no more make a choice to do something that doesn't follow a line of code than I can grow wings and fly, but when you give it a girl's voice people lose their minds," I told him with a smile. "Annie doesn't think, so she's not artificial intelligence. She can't make choices like a human can."

The guy was flustered but accepted it all the same.

"So why give it a female voice and call it 'her'?" he asked.

"Because a perceived personality, especially a female one with a nice voice, makes people comfortable. It's just how we're wired up," I told him with a smile, regurgitating the lines I'd practiced for years.

Truth was, I'd intentionally stayed well away from the AI world, as that shit scares the hell out of me. I think I'd watched that old movie about computers becoming self-aware once too often as a kid, and remember having had nightmares about everything electrical coming to life to try and kill all the humans. Stupid really, as Annie could no more decide to eradicate the human race than I could make her think for herself. It was science fiction, and not the kind that becomes science fact. At least that was what I thought.

Recovering, the guy checked the reply showing on his cell phone before answering rapidly with both thumbs and then slipping it away in a pocket. He straightened his suit jacket before hitting me with his best corporate smile. "Well, Mr. Weatherby is very happy with your answers, and he would like you to bring the ANII and all of your work to Texas." He stood, indicating that the brief meeting was over.

"Sure," I said, "when?"

"Right now."

Company Space Research Center, Texas
December 1, 2021

Amir Weatherby was on the tarmac to greet the flustered genius prodigy programmer brought in from their eastern European research facility. The rush to pack everything and climb aboard a company helicopter was still fresh in the young man's mind, even after the opulence of the private jet that transported him directly to the US.

Amir wore a crisply tailored two-piece suit despite the heat, and he smiled a winning smile.

"Dr. Anderson," he said warmly, "David. It's a pleasure to see you again, this way, please," he said after a handshake that must have been coached by at least one former president. Anderson followed him inside and escaped the stifling heat which threatened to take his breath away after the sub-zero temperatures of winter in Estonia. Pleasantries were exchanged as they walked, passing other suited men and women and a number of fit-looking people in tan combat trousers and black polo shirts. Anderson answered automatically as he took in the surroundings and suddenly felt very shabby, like they had dusted off the crazy computer geek for some kind of attraction, and

17

found his eyes lingering on the lower back of a woman wearing the unmarked uniform of the site security team. Glancing behind her, she saw his eyes dart back up to her face with a look of shock, then returned it with a look of distain as she turned away.

I wasn't checking out your ass, Anderson thought to himself, *I was looking at the gun. And who the hell hides their guns in Texas, anyway?*

The telltale bulge in the small of her back clearly held something under the shirt, and as he looked at the others wearing the same tan and black combo with their pants tucked into their desert boots, he saw a lot more poorly concealed weaponry.

Their small talk ended as the door to a conference room opened up ahead. Amir stood in the doorway and took a long breath as he prepared for his intelligence to make a brilliant appearance. Starting from left to right, he introduced each of the twenty or so people sat at the large table including their personal areas of expertise. Anderson knew none of them, recognized maybe three of the faces, and remembered none of their names. He was invited to sit, which he did, and ran through what he considered to be the important facts.

Geology, meteorology, astronomy, physics, cryogenics, ecology, oceanography, biology, genetics, botany … the list of scientific achievements was incredible, and no less than three Nobel Prize nominees were in the room. On top of the scientists were some rugged looking men and women, including a human resources manager called Hayley Cole. She had apparently revolutionized many state run departments and private companies before Amir had offered her more money than she would make in the rest of her life to advise him personally. She was maybe thirty, severe looking but still very feminine, albeit in a kind of hard way. She wore a pant suit tailored to her form, the form of a runner by the look of her, and she exuded confidence with a good dose of dominance in a world ruled over by men.

There were also a handful of men whose simple demeanor screamed their military backgrounds from the rooftops, and one of them was introduced as their resident expert survivalist.

Quite why they had survivalists with military careers in a conference room with scientists responsible for the genetic mutation of crops to allow sustainable food to be grown in drought-ridden parts of Africa was beyond Anderson, as was his own inclusion in the elite gathering.

"Ladies and gentlemen," Amir said confidently as he undid the single button of his suit jacket with forefinger and thumb smoothly as he sat. Anderson was caught on that simple act, the gesture which Amir Weatherby did a hundred times a day and came so naturally to him that he had no idea how utterly privileged it made him seem, that he missed the first few words he spoke.

"… a think-tank if you like, where all of you have a specific element to input to the project. As you know, all of your research and works are well funded by our companies, so I'd like for you to consider this your highest priority. Just one thing before we begin," he said solemnly, "if you would all please open the binder in front of you"—Anderson noticed the leather-bound folder on the desk which looked like a menu in a very expensive restaurant—"and read the first document. It is a strict non-disclosure agreement, and you are all consenting to not discuss the subject matter of this project with anyone who is not subject to the same agreement. I cannot be any clearer about this," he finished, leaving a small sense of feeling stunned wafting around the room. One by one they all read and signed the non-disclosure forms, Anderson finding that his own already bore his name and listed that any breach of the signed agreement would result in the immediate termination of the project named ANII, as well as an enforced seizure of all intellectual property rights and research materials associated to it, with the added kicker of a very thorough non-compete clause.

Serious stuff.

Well, it's not like I actually talk to many people anyway, Anderson thought to himself with a resigned sadness as he scribbled his name. Eventually, all of the documents were signed, either immediately or with a degree of trepidation. No doubt each of them stood to lose out significantly if they breached the agreement, but none were willing to walk away from this exciting new theme. The human resources—Cole—woman collected the papers, her careful eyes scanning each one for anyone who signed their name as Mickey Mouse, and nodded once to Amir as she shuffled the papers into a single, neat stack.

"Now that's out of the way," Amir said seriously, "the problem I want you to discuss and formulate working theories on is this: Imagine an asteroid will hit the earth in ten years' time and will be a more destructive event than the one that killed the dinosaurs by a factor of four."

With that, he sat back and watched the mouths of everyone at the table fall open.

Chapter 3

Company Space Research Center, Texas
June 18, 2022

"We know it's going to hit, and we know it's going to be ninety-five percent plus," said their astronomy expert tiredly as he sat to rub the bridge of his nose.

"You can't make that extinction prediction, Kenneth," said the geologist, "not until we know the landfall of it. If it's in the mid-Atlantic then that's one thing, but if it hits North America then the whole planet is gone if Yellowstone blows."

Anderson leaned back and let out an exasperated groan which silenced them. Finding a common enemy, the warring scientists turned on the lowly computer programmer.

"Something to say, *Dr.* Anderson?" asked Professor Kenneth Howard, the team's foremost expert on all things cryogenic.

Jesus, this again? Anderson thought.

"Yes actually," he said, "I do. The difference between ninety and one hundred percent is irrelevant," he said earning scoffing noises from the others, "because if this happened then we would need to either safely store on Earth, or store in orbit a repository of everything we need: seeds, animals, humans, manufacturing resources for resettlement and repopulation."

This was the fundamental difference in the two main trends of thinking amongst them. They had been working almost daily for six months on the problem, and Anderson leaned heavily toward the concept of hibernation.

He had embarrassed himself the first time they had discussed the extinction percentages, offering the opinion that five to ten percent of life surviving the impact seemed pretty good to him, only to be laughed at to learn that the percentages they were discussing were the extinction rates of the impact alone, and not the survival rates after the ensuing ice age and rapid warming as the planet's atmosphere fluctuated dangerously. After that, they all agreed on a figure somewhere between ninety-nine and one hundred percent.

He glanced down to his final written report which had been requested from all of them by the end of that week. They were supposed to have been written independently after a half-year of discussions among the experts in their fields. He had little to offer to many people, but when the cryogenics expert, Elliot Whitmore, discussed how their technology, albeit in its very early stages of development, still needed human operation to make it work, that was where he and Annie came in. The two of them now offered and almost identical report.

"Working on the concept that you would need a minimum of one hundred and sixty human beings of reproductive age to provide the capability to restart the human race, then selecting those people and storing them cryogenically in orbit would negate any of the harmful effects of the asteroid's impact and allow them to return to the planet to rebuild, along with all of the plant and animal life they would require to become self-sufficient within a year."

He liked the plan, as did others, and all it would take were the giant space station and cryopods along with about fifty years to program Annie, the resources they needed, and a list of one hundred and sixty people. He loved theory, but he was becoming bored with the delay in developing his masterpiece and wanted to go back to his cold research facility again.

The end of the week came and went, and they had the weekend to rest before they were summoned to the conference room once more. Amir was there, this time flanked by two new people that Anderson hadn't seen before. He introduced them as Ian Edwards, formerly of JPL and NASA and now the company's space program manager, and Mr. Tanaka, who was introduced simply as his chief of security.

Anderson, luckily within the safe confines of his own mind, instantly decided that the scowling Mr. Tanaka was an asshole. He was about forty, Asian American in appearance and accent, and he struck the computer scientist as a man utterly without humor. The chief of security glowered at each and every person at the table, offering the most reluctant of greetings as though he were expecting an assassination attempt at any point. Anderson's attention was snatched back to the real world when Amir started speaking.

"As everyone at this table is here because of their intellect, I doubt that any of you still think that this is just a theoretical exercise," he said, pausing to survey the shifting looks of discomfort among the audience. "I can tell you now that the event you have been planning for is an inevitability," he finished, just as the room erupted with a dozen questions at once. Holding up both hands and waiting for calm order to restore itself, Amir's face showed no hostility or defensiveness, merely the professional outlook that he approached every task with.

"Ladies and gentlemen, please," he said as Mr. Tanaka shifted uneasily beside him with his right hand worryingly and surreptitiously out of sight behind his back. "Ladies and gentlemen," Amir said louder this time, regaining control of the room, "everything you know about the exercise is what we know about the asteroid. It will hit the earth on January 20, 2033 and it will wipe out everything," he said, waiting for the fact to sink in.

"It goes without saying that everyone in this room will be included in any plan to survive, as will your families," Amir announced, seeing relief bathe half of the scientists.

Either half of them don't have families, Anderson thought to himself, *or they really are heartless sons of bitches.*

"I have read your reports," Amir continued, "and I know what the effects of the impact will be, so we are enacting two of the suggested plans. As you know, we have acquired the International Space Station due to dwindling government funding, and we are beginning the process of retrofitting it. Ian?" he said, deferring to the other newcomer beside him. Ian Edwards cleared his throat and stepped forward.

"As of today, the ISS is being redesigned as the Automated Resettlement and Repopulation Cryostation, or *Ark* as the ARC acronym so aptly suggests. As fitting as the name is, the redesign is huge and will require numerous trips to space for the work to be carried out. Whilst you have been working on the survivability issue, we have designed an affordable transport method which relies on the use of balloons to get the materials into space by way of capsules, and the capsules will be remote piloted to the ARC. The capsules will be pre-fabricated here on Earth, then sent up to be added to the station."

"How do we get our people up there? Are we freezing them down here and sending them up?" asked Elliot, the closest thing Anderson had to a friend in the group and their cryogenics expert.

"That's still being considered," Edwards answered carefully, "but yes, it's likely that we will put the majority of people into cryostasis down here and transport them in that state both to and from the ARC. That way we don't have to stress them with space flight and zero-G training."

"What about power?" asked their physicist.

Edwards glanced to Amir and Tanaka, who in turn glanced at each other until Tanaka shrugged. Edwards turned back to the table.

"We have acquired three CNRs, compact nuclear reactors, and one of them will be attached to the ARC to supplement the solar arrays."

The person asking the question nodded and began to scribble notes on their pad, obviously satisfied that additional power sources were being considered. Anderson noticed that there was no mention of the other two reactors but bypassed the fact as it dawned on him what his role in the plan was.

He would need to program Annie to run the space station, to control the cryopods, to remote pilot modules to and from Earth, to interpret data on a dozen subjects he hadn't programmed her for yet, and probably a dozen more that he hadn't even considered yet.

"I need to reiterate," Amir announced seriously as he fixed everyone in turn with direct eye contact, "that any details of the impending ... problem ... and your parts in the solution for it *Must.*

Not. Leave. This. Facility," he said as he jabbed a finger onto the table top with each emphasized word. "Now, you will all be given specific assignments for development, so please continue, and be assured that, together, we will survive this," he finished with a smile. The occupants of the room melted away, some to huddle into discussions with each other and some to their own thoughts. The news that their theory exercise was actually a reality came as no major shock to any of them, but the truth of their suspicions offered little or no comfort now that it was confirmed as a fact.

"Dr. Anderson?" Amir said, startling him. "Might I have a word?"

Nodding dumbly, Anderson stood and followed him out of the room with Tanaka and Edwards trailing behind.

I don't know what I was thinking right then. I guess I was in a bit of shock at being told the asteroid was going to destroy Earth, and for some stupid reason I couldn't get the imagery from some Hollywood film out of my head. I was trying to decide whether suggesting that we fly a team to it and set off nukes was a good idea, when I remembered that the popular opinion was that the thing was just too damn big to destroy, and instead of one asteroid we'd end up creating a half dozen or more.

It was like choosing whether to be shot with a rifle or a shotgun; both were bad options.

As I followed Amir to his office, I found myself getting pissed at Tanaka who was walking just a little too close behind me for my liking. The guy was menacing when I could see him but sensing him there in my blind spot made my neck crawl. Luckily, we got to where we were going, and he didn't follow us in but just stayed outside like a bodyguard.

Walking into the office I saw two guys I'd never met before, and both looked up at me expectantly.

"David Anderson," Amir said in a clipped, businesslike tone, "meet Christopher Eades and John Kendall."

I nodded to both of the guys. The one called Kendall offered me a kind of nod that made me think the guy was a douchebag. The eyes were cocky, and the chin just flicked up like the guy was saying *s'up*. I looked at the other guy who stood up, showing that he was a lot taller than me but built like a bamboo cane. He offered me his hand and spoke in a British accent which surprised me for a second.

"Pleasure to meet you, Dr. Anderson," he said formally as I clasped his hand back tightly. "I must confess that I am a fan of your work," he finished as he let go and took his seat again.

"Er, thanks," I said, feeling inadequate.

"I'll get to the point again," Amir said from behind the desk as the keyboard tapped to the rhythm of him inputting his personal credentials. "John here works in the US-based part of the company in network security, and Christopher is from our UK office where he develops new software. I want both to work with you, and both to have a basic version of the ANII for programming. All three of you will have different roles to play, so each of you will move off in different directions when the time comes," Amir said as he finished typing a long password and looked up at me directly.

"I don't like reiterating what sounds like a threat, but nothing we discuss can be repeated to anyone who isn't here right now, is that understood?"

All three of us mumbled our assurances that we understood him. The Edwards guy stood in the corner and said nothing, obviously his silence was already a done deal.

"David," Amir said to me again, "you will program your ANII for the space station. Christopher will program his for a repository in Europe, and John will program his for a site on the African continent which is being excavated as we speak."

I opened my mouth to ask more about both sites but managed to swallow the words before they escaped. I decided I'd ask the Brit and the douchebag when we weren't in front of the boss.

"So," Amir asked, "what do you need?"

I fought down the childish jealousy I suddenly felt. I wanted to keep Annie for myself, and the thought of giving away two copies of her to people I didn't know was like having to pick my favorite child and give away the others. Luckily, good sense and reason managed to poke its head into my thoughts and I created the shopping list in my head.

I told him what I needed, listing off everything as he typed. He glanced back up at me whenever he caught up with what I was asking for. I decided to try and lighten the mood by asking for a brandy glass full of red M&Ms each morning to be left in my dressing room, and only Eades laughed. Amir smiled politely at my joke, but I got the impression that he didn't actually find me very funny. He told me that he would get everything, then opened a drawer and pulled out three keycards bearing our names on one each.

"Lab K has been assigned for you," he said as he offered me the cards, "I'm sure you can find it and get started. Gentlemen," he finished, dismissing us with the polite manner that seemed to leak from his skin.

In truth, I was still reeling a little to learn that there were two other projects running as well as the space station idea. No doubt other suggestions were agreed from our individual recommendations, and then I was kind of in a slow tailspin that I was actually the asshole who was getting shot out into space to wait for the world to calm down again. That was basically the plan: hide or run away, wait in the freezer until the earth was a safe place again, and go back to start over. I wasn't much of a conspiracy theory guy, and I also wasn't one for disaster movies, so hearing the level of destruction we were facing was kind of an eye-opener.

Here's what I understood would happen to the planet after spending six months with the other geeks:

There was an asteroid, not a meteor or a comet apparently, not that I cared much for the distinction, that was about ninety miles across heading for Earth travelling at a little over thirty thousand miles an hour. Now that sounded real fast to me, but realizing that it's so far away and will still take a decade to get here makes you feel a little small in the universe.

When it does eventually get here, it will hit us. I listened to hours and hours of arguing over whether the sun will pull it closer with its gravitational field and make it miss, but of all the dozens of calculations they did, only one model had the thing missing the planet. So, we concluded, it was coming.

When it hits us, and hopefully by that time I'll be a human popsicle in space, it will kill almost everything on Earth with the impact. It'll be like thirty billion Hiroshimas in one go as all that energy is released, all those thousands if not hundreds of thousands of years spent hurtling through space on the longest joyride ever would end abruptly as the kinetic energy met our little planet. It'll smash through our atmosphere blasting a huge hole, it'll superheat with the friction of the air resisting it, and it will go boom into the surface leaving a crater close to six hundred miles wide.

The one thing the other geeks couldn't agree on is where the thing will hit. Now that has something to do with not being able to predict the gravitational pull of the sun in a decade, but either way, we still needed to evacuate the building.

One guy kept going on and on about Yellowstone, about how if it hits that it'll erase the entire US, but he was kind of on his own. They did concede that active volcanoes would go off when the thing impacts, but the general feel was that it couldn't get much worse than it already was; it was like discussing degrees of total destruction, and nobody really took it seriously. Where everyone did agree though, is what happened after an impact either in an ocean or near to any coastal region. Anything not flattened by the blast would get hit by the waves. Tsunamis would reach three or four hundred miles inland and any landfall at sea level would disappear. All the debris and dust and other shit from the impact would make a cloud big enough to cover the earth and block out the sun; we're talking somewhere in the region of two hundred billion tons of debris. No sun means no photosynthesis, which means no plants, which means no animals, which means no higher life forms.

That's what will kill anything that doesn't go out like a light on impact.

The cloud covering the earth will be full of things like iridium and mercury, all good stuff to breathe in, and the planet would find itself in a nuclear winter which would last twenty or thirty years, or more, until the cloud dissipated. During that winter, the surface temperature would freeze and the planet would go into an ice age.

Years later, when the ash and debris settle out of the sky, and the sunlight gets back in, that's when things get real uncomfortable; the extreme cold gets replaced with extreme heat as all the carbon still pumped into the atmosphere acts like a glasshouse and the surface temperature rockets to the other end of the thermometer. That heatwave bakes the earth for years until it finally settles down. So basically, it makes the earth either too *exploding*, too cold, or too hot for life to survive, then it returns to a state of balance. Just like the dinosaurs sixty-five million years ago, only bigger and badder.

And they sure as hell weren't going to find *my* blood in a mosquito preserved in amber.

Those facts didn't make life any easier to accept, but they simplified the problem. The solution, however, was far from simple, as I explained to the others as we walked to lab K in the Texas facility. I started with the basics of how Annie worked. She was fundamentally an interface system with connectivity through every means available to us: cellular, Wi-Fi, radio, etcetera. There was a basic central processing program which I'd spent years developing, and that basic program was now at a stage where it could be told to do virtually anything. That basic program was already running the drone delivery system and the manufacturing and packaging plants, and the only human intervention was at the quality control stage.

I explained how she worked to the others, and where Eades was keen, Kendall looked almost bored. Annie basically worked like a flowchart, and the idea was one that I got years ago in high school when I saw one of those stupid pictures. It went something like: Is it broken? With a yes or no option flowing down. The 'No' option told you to leave it alone, whereas the 'Yes' option told you to pretend you didn't see it. While the joke was a poor one, the concept had gotten me thinking.

Could a computer program follow a flowchart? Of course it could, you only need to input the options and the parameters for choosing each one. It was the closest approximation to human thinking from a computer, which is why I called her a non-sentient intelligence interface. She is non-sentient because the choices she makes are human-programmed choices, which give her the appearance of a true AI without the possibility of that higher-thinking thing where the machines decide to do away with us meat-sacks. The downside of the system I had designed was that each and every possible outcome or decision had to be identified, placed into the flowchart which is how I recorded the programming language, and coded into Annie's language.

Simple, yet time consuming. I'd already guessed that I'd need more years to program everything than we had, but as deadlines went this one was pretty solid.

Chapter 4

Amir Weatherby's helicopter landed amidst a roiling storm of dust blown up by the arrival of the disruptive rotary blades. The pilot powered down as soon as the wheels cushioned their landing, and the occupants waited for a few minutes to allow themselves to exit into air that was more gas than solid dust.

When the orange-colored cloud dissipated, the rear sliding door opened to reveal Amir wearing more casual, hot weather clothing rather than his characteristic tailored suits. He had withdrawn slightly from the limelight of international publicity of late, and told the world in a short press conference that he was spending more time focusing on family as his mother's health was a concern. He thanked everyone for their kindness and understanding, asked the international press to respect his family's wishes for privacy, and left without taking any questions.

Now, wearing simple khaki chinos with boat shoes and a white polo shirt, he stepped down and swept off his shades as he walked into the shadow of the facility entrance. He was fascinated by the explanations given by the team of structural engineers, about how they had built an entrance to the facility, but given its limitations and the stresses that the structure would be expected to endure, the plan for anyone getting out of it would be to abandon their route in and tunnel a new exit. With that in mind, the main chamber of the top level of the bunker was as cavernous as a football stadium, where the excess earth and rock from their exit could be deposited.

The place was alive with a local workforce scurrying like ants under the leadership of the engineers. Amir and his small procession were led down steel staircases to the lower levels, of which he knew from the plans that there were eighteen. The site itself was carefully chosen from a shortlist of appropriate areas where the expected tectonic plate shift would leave the region undisturbed, and the added bonus was that it was in a region where the company held some element of authority thanks to the long-established support for the mining of precious stones and minerals.

Also, ever the businessman, Amir knew that the labor costs were low and the authorities were easily corruptible. Greed made a person predictable, he knew.

Ranks of reinforced cables lined the stairwell, each encased in metal cages to protect them, and they were reminded to watch their footing as they descended.

"I need you folks to wear these from here on in," said Miles Hawthorn, the big engineer in charge of the project, as he pointed to a rack of mining-style hardhats and yellow vests. Amir had found him working on oil drilling equipment as part of a merger deal and had liked his forthright style. Putting on his own helmet and activating the light, he led them onwards to a lower level where the lighting was dull. He pulled the entourage aside as a group and gave them his safety speech.

"Alright folks, at all times you stay behind me and you stay in line. As of now I am number one, and you are two, three, four, five, and six, you got that?" he asked after pointing to each of them in turn. "I shout *ONE*, and you sound off in turn, that way we know if anyone gets lost in the dark. I'll tell you again, this is a *working site*, and I cannot guarantee your safety if you don't follow my instructions. We clear?"

They were clear, and Amir smiled to himself in the dark as they set off dutifully like ducks in a row into the depths. He had inspected the European site and found a similar construction, if a little smaller and less hectic than Hawthorn's project in Africa seemed. He could hardly visit the third site, not easily anyway, but he had toured the construction units in Texas where the pods were painstakingly manufactured before shipping to another part of the complex for the installation of the cryopods. Testing on the freezers, as people were calling them, had been escalated massively with volunteers going into stasis each month until they were thawed out and given rigorous physical and psychological testing to check for varying results. The first to spend an entire year in cryostasis was woken up only the month before, and after a day of dizziness and nausea he seemed no worse for the experience.

Stepping back into the present as he stumbled on a loose piece of rock, he concentrated on his footing as they hit level five of the underground complex.

"Basically, as you know," Hawthorn said loudly in the echoing confines of the underground chamber, "the facility is a reinforced steel and concrete pod constructed inside the softer earth. Any movement of the plates here should allow the pod to stay intact and as undisturbed as possible. The power source is down at level twelve, and that powers the whole show for the lights and the freezers ..."

"Are you on schedule?" Amir interrupted, knowing the schematics of the facility better than most. Hawthorn stopped to regard him, illuminating his face with the torch on his hardhat and making him squint his eyes.

"Yes," he said with a hint of pride, "actually we are about a month and a half ahead at the moment."

That pleased Amir. His company's unexpected overt move into mineral mining was the official cover story for their massive excavations, and the well-paid militia kept any prying eyes out of the site along with the blackout on satellite coverage.

Which was actually fairly easy to do when you owned not only the software, but also the satellites that everyone's smartphones relied on.

"What's the timeline for pod installation?" Amir asked.

"Six months to start, eighteen to finish," Hawthorn responded immediately. "Construction isn't really the issue here, it's the wiring that takes the longest at this stage, and after the installation everything catches up real quick. The big question I was expecting was when can we get the reactor installed …"

"It is being delivered in a little over three months, mid-May time, and will be activated within six weeks from there so, Mr. Hawthorn, you'll have your endless power supply before the pods arrive."

Hawthorn smiled at his employer. "Well that suits me just fine."

The tour continued, with each level being addressed by its intended function and purpose in the grand scheme. Amir marveled at the willingness and alacrity that people working on these projects, at least those in the knowledge of why they were doing it, possessed.

Perhaps the impending eradication of all life on Earth was the drive necessary to finally get a dedicated and committed workforce.

The plan for the large bunker project was simple. Close to five hundred people would be selected and frozen down there, with endless supplies of energy on tap from one of their three compact nuclear reactors. The plan, after their solid bubble under the earth regains consciousness and the occupants tunnel outward to repopulate the earth, will be to begin the process of 'defrosting' their main cargo over a period of time. This facility, being the biggest by far, was intended to hold the majority of the livestock animals of all types and breeds. It was hardly two by two, but the genetics teams were hard at work producing the best specimens and ensuring their fertility before shipping them off for cryostasis.

Perhaps because the animals underwent no psychological testing after their test freezes, or perhaps because they were just less able to demonstrate any complaint, they seemed almost entirely untouched by the process and recovered within minutes in some cases.

The geneticists were also hard at work on the other living cargo to be transported into the future, and each member of the teams who had secured a place on either the ARC or the two bunkers were subjected to rigorous testing.

The second bunker, again built in a country where prying eyes could be kept away and interested governments could be easily diverted through their obvious financial priorities, was on a smaller scale but was still intended to hold livestock, plant specimens, materials and equipment, as well as their human specimens. Just as the ARC, which would be sent out to deep earth orbit so that it wouldn't be close enough to suffer from the impact blast or the ensuing radiation problems, the other two projects to ensure the survival of humanity were intended as individual redundancies in case either of the others failed. Each of the three systems operated slightly differently, as different as deep underground and far out in space could be. It was hoped that all three could survive the holocaust coming in eight years, but each *could* survive independently if the worst should happen.

This was Amir Weatherby's entire life now, as he circled the globe to keep tabs on each individual part of the plan to save humanity. He felt grateful to regain the open air above, just as he simultaneously regretted the sweltering heat of the African sun. He had spent much of his life in India so was no stranger to hot weather, but the lack of humidity made him feel as though his body was visibly drying out whenever he was in direct sunshine there. Boarding the helicopter with a wave to Hawthorn, the engines screamed into life and the rotor blades began to spin lazily above his head. Just as they spun up to an intensity where no single shape was visible in the whirring circle of shadow above him, the ground dropped away as the pilot launched them skywards and north to the airstrip where his modest but luxurious Bombardier Global sat refueled and ready for his next destination. He sweated in the confines of the expensive helicopter and closed his eyes to imagine the change of clothes and ice-cold water waiting for him on his arrival.

That arrival, forty uncomfortable minutes later, did not bear the relief he was expecting.

Chapter 5

Texas

February 10, 2025

I felt like a lab rat. I felt like I wasn't the scientist, but that I was the subject being studied to see just how much repetitive work one man could do before he grew a wild beard, talked to himself all the time, and eventually went nuts and murdered everyone else in the facility.

I'd done my fair share of lab work, hell, I missed being shut away in the freezing cold in Estonia, but this was intense.

Every day I get up to an alarm, usually about three hours after finally getting to sleep despite falling into bed every single day feeling exhausted. I do thirty minutes of exercise straight away before eating or drinking, then chug down a big glass of water before hitting the shower. I get dressed, I eat breakfast, and I hit the lab.

All day, every day, I program Annie with the controls for this and that or something else. Every day I have to answer questions from the annoying Kendall or the overly polite Eades, and every day I go just a little more insane. It was okay for the first few months, when I was giving the language coding lessons to them, but after that they went to their separate labs and I never saw them. I never saw anyone much, and the quacks here realized that I just fall into a hole when I'm working alone so they send someone in with lunch to talk to me.

It's usually a pretty girl because, you know, I'm a guy, and they obviously don't want me going insane, so they reckon on me acting like a human being if they put me in a room with someone that my primitive senses tell me I can breed with, and I'll behave. They chose well. She was about my age but a head shorter, and she was warm and quick to smile where other women there frightened me a little. I couldn't place her mix of ethnicity with her dark hair and eyes but smooth light brown skin, and despite my need to analyze and break down information to its composite parts I felt rude to ask her without getting to know her first. She had none of the flinty-hardness that others exuded. Instead she was both welcoming and quietly alluring without being some overt symbol of misogynistic rule. I found myself instantly liking her, but never taking her presence for granted. She introduced herself simply as Cat and assumed her daily responsibilities of keeping me sane as though she had always been doing it.

It worked. Every day. But as soon as my companionable waitress left, no doubt to go and report on me, I lapsed back into the black hole of work. After a month on my own, they tried to give me a lab assistant. That didn't last because the idiot tried to ask me questions to understand what I was doing. I didn't need to have to explain the basics of interactive computer interfaces to a novice, so I politely threw his ass out.

It wasn't the usual interfacing issues that were grinding my patience and my mind to dust, it was feeding Annie the operating procedures manual for the cryopod system one line at a time. Converting the manual to code was relatively easy, but actually inputting it was not; each line I added was assessed and profiled by Annie's operating system, and a single symbol or number out of place made her understanding of that line of code get thrown out. Her 'mind' operates like a process, so if there's one bad link in the chain then all hell could break loose.

And I was pretty sure I wasn't the only one who didn't want all hell breaking loose when I was in human popsicle form.

My wandering mind was becoming a problem for productivity, I decided, just as the buzzer sounded to indicate that I was done for the day. I always ignored it, finishing the section of coding I was working on to prevent any assimilation issues. Just my luck, that day I was only about twenty percent into the section, so I'd be there for another hour at least.

As I finished the section of coding, I rubbed by eyes and pushed my wheeled chair back away from the desk to slide across the room and pick up the manual.

"Yo, Annie," I said. I heard her answering beep and looked at the section of the manual I had just inputted. "What would you do if a pod shows a malfunction at T plus five hundred and nine?" I asked, plucking a random number out of the air to test the coding. I looked at the speaker installed on the wall and heard the tone which indicated Annie was working. Or *thinking*, as I liked to call it.

She knew what I meant by 'pods' or 'stasis units' or 'cryotubes' or any of two dozen ways of referring to the freezers because I had programmed her with an ability to access and search synonyms in a fraction of a second. Actually, she would have known what I meant by freezers too.

Another beep told me she had the answer, and I leaned back to hear her thoughts on the subject.

"In the event of pod malfunction," she said using the same vernacular as the person asking the question, "after one year, four months, three weeks, one day, five hours, forty-six minutes and thirty-nine seconds, would result in me notifying the on-duty maintenance team," she said, making me slide back to the keyboard and input a general code line into the response sub-menu to limit the accuracy of her answers unless accuracy was specifically asked for.

"And if you couldn't raise the on-duty maintenance team?" I prompted, imaging not the flowchart of what anyone would do next, but instead the lines of code I had inputted giving her the options and which parameters should dictate the one she chose.

"Have the on-duty maintenance team been rendered inactive or injured?" she asked, seeking the information she needed to complete the process.

"No, they just aren't answering," I told her.

"In the event of pod malfunction after five hundred and nine days in stasis, and if the on-duty maintenance team were not responsive but not injured or incapacitated, I would wait until subject viability is likely to become impaired before initiating the resuscitation process myself."

"Thanks, Annie. I'm going now, see you tomorrow," I told her as I stood and walked for the door stretching my back.

"Goodnight, David," said the speaker on the wall. "Sleep well," she added making me stop in my tracks.

"Annie, identify last line of code," I said, with no idea when I programmed in that personal response. Her beeps told me she was thinking before she answered, "I'm sorry, I'm unable to respond."

"Annie," I said again carefully, "define user who programmed response to 'see you tomorrow.'"

"I'm sorry, I'm unable to respond."

I was torn between returning to the terminal to dig through about a billion lines of code until I found it, or letting it go. It's not like Annie telling me to sleep well was weird, or a problem, but I couldn't remember ever coding that response. I was eventually to realize that it was Annie who had created that response herself.

Bah, it was probably Dr. Douchebag, I thought to myself as I swiped my way out of the lab to get some food before a hot bath.

John 'Douchebag' Kendall wasn't the problem. Christopher Eades, the polite British computer scientist whose impeccable manners and overwhelming sense of propriety charmed, if not confused, most Americans, was doing what could only be described as *meddling*.

Whilst he was brought in as a foremost expert in computer programming, a talent he had learned later in life and found himself displaying a flair for, his doctorate and former work had been in the field of genetics. His vision, not one that he publicly shared for fear of being treated like a madman by those without the foresight to understand his goals, was a simple one in essence.

He wanted to tame, or domesticate, a species of animal. Just like man has done with dogs for thousands of years, he had a vision of a team of animal workers which could construct and follow orders perfectly. A workforce that did not tire, that needed little in the way of sustenance, and never complained about long working hours or employee rights. He wanted an army of creatures, equally able to construct and to defend should the need arise.

He experimented with ants but found that their natural aggression was too difficult to tame. He tried a series of other insects, some failures due to his inability to grow them large enough and others due to their inability to receive and understand commands. Returning slightly to his original idea, he genetically crossed the large species of Bullet ants with a fast, strong breed of beetle, the Tiger. After years of testing, he was close to creating a computerized control of the hive queen and was on the verge of being able to program her to give her orders to the army of hybrid bugs he envisioned.

That's when he got the call from Amir Weatherby, asking him to meet.

He had taken that job in a second and kept his own personal plans very close to his chest. Living at the European site from the time the first ground was broken, he continued his programming of the ANII as well as his own research, having procured a set of the smaller cryounits used for preserving animal species. He had planned a small adjustment to the facility, requesting approval for a secure off-site storage facility feeding off their own nuclear power source, and he stored his own secret project there, ready to colonize with dominance when they regained the surface of the earth.

As with all narcissists, he truly believed what he was doing was for the good of humanity.

Chapter 6

Central Africa
February 10, 2025

"Good afternoon, gentlemen," Amir said as he stepped down from the helicopter and walked toward the two very uncomfortable looking men in dull suit pants and shirts with unbuttoned collars and rolled-up sleeves. The two obvious government types, all mass-produced service weapons and polyester suits, had clearly been waiting somewhere without air conditioning, which meant that they had been denied access to the private lounge he used whenever he had to visit the region. That told him that their badges held no sway and prompted no fear here.

Neither spoke as he approached, his entourage hesitantly flocking close, but not too close, behind him.

"I trust you have been offered refreshments while you waited for me?" he asked politely, intending to insult them with impeccable manners. "Please, come inside."

He climbed the steps to the low building, nonchalantly waving a hand as the armed security personnel granted him access immediately. The suits glanced once at each other and followed. The fact that neither wore shades, nor had been dressed for the occasion, the occasion being Africa, told Amir that they had been sent in a hurry.

Taking a seat and holding up a hand in a lazy gesture which was both oozing with privilege and subtly stylish in manner, he watched as a uniformed waitress scurried off to return with his mineral water and ice.

"And two more for my friends, please," he added, indicating the sweat-stained and tired men. "Please, gentlemen, sit down."

Both sat, obviously eager to be in the cool interior and happily accepting their ice-waters, whilst trying to keep their best game faces on having located their target.

"So, *Agents,*" Amir said with relish, "what can I do for you?"

The slightly taller of the two non-descript men sipped his drink and leaned back to regard the sleek private jet sat on the tarmac, as though that was some form of answer.

"Okay," Amir said, "I shall guess. CIA or Homeland?"

The men glanced at each other and smirked, enjoying that he had got it wrong.

"Well I know the NSA has assets here who are better suited to make any approach to me, and the director of the FBI has my personal cell phone number," he said without a trace of arrogance, which was an arrogance in itself, but one borne of power.

Still neither said anything.

"Which only leaves," Amir said with a little more steel in his voice, "the Treasury department or DoD …" He sipped his drink and crossed his legs with his right ankle on his left knee to regard both men. They knew he had the facts straight, and to reveal which one of the agencies they were from would be to tell him what they wanted. Still, neither said anything.

"Very well," Amir went on as he drained his drink and stood, "I am returning to the United States now, so unless you are detaining an American citizen in a non-extradition country without a warrant, I bid you good day." With that he nodded to them and walked toward the exit doors.

"We're DoD," said one of them in an unmistakable New York accent, "and our boss would like a word with you."

"The secretary of defense, or the president?" Amir asked as he turned, meaning to enquire as to which boss they meant.

"SecDef, sir," the other one answered with more deference. "What we know hasn't reached the White House," he said before adding an ominous, "yet."

"Very well," Amir said, "is your jet on standby or shall we take mine?"

The move to intimidate the two bothered agents by transporting them in luxury worked, in that both had to repeatedly turn down drinks of expensive and rare alcohol during the long flight west. Of all the acronyms in the US, the DoD were the shadiest of all when it came to what they were and weren't allowed to do by law. When they had the scent of something, they didn't allow such annoyances as a person's constitutional rights to impede them in achieving their goals.

The two agents said nothing the entire flight, after one of them had smiled at Amir as soon as the pilot had announced their expected arrival time in Virginia.

"I bet you're wondering how we found you?" the younger agent asked mockingly.

"Yes, I did wonder that," Amir said casually, "after all, I only used my own personal jet from a commercial US airport after passing through customs with my passport and lodging the flight plan with the Federal Aviation Administration," he answered with a smile meaning to explain that he left a trail of breadcrumbs that a child on their first day in local law enforcement could have followed. He sipped his cognac and allowed himself an internal smile of victory.

Virginia, USA
February 11, 2025

Touching down early the following morning, Amir Weatherby left the plane wearing a crisp three-piece and a form-fitting coat, exquisitely tailored as ever, and walked fast down the airplane steps with a casual spring. In contrast, the two agents emerged blinking into the early morning light wearing the same clothes they had worn for a little over two days and barely registering any sleep to speak of. Amir left instructions for the rest of his entourage to clear the runway and fly back to Texas as soon as he had left.

Walking directly to the second of four large, armored Escalades, Amir opened the rear door and climbed in as the man in the back seat slid over to the passenger side.

"Mr. Secretary," Amir said offering a hand, "I assume we aren't going to your office?"

"Mr. Weatherby," responded the ageing, retired general sharing the back seat with him, "no, I think we can find somewhere more private than that." With that, the convoy peeled out, as the two exhausted delivery boys climbed tiredly into the rear vehicle.

"I'll get right to the point, Weatherby," Secretary of Defense Matthews said as he sat heavily in the chair opposite the much younger man, "we know you've imported radioactive material stateside," he said, leaving the statement open for response.

Amir sipped his coffee before responding with a question.

"And what would you believe this *radioactive material* to be, Mr. Secretary?"

Matthews stared hard at him, thinking that he was a little upstart of a shit-nugget who inherited the keys to the kingdom from his daddy, and his daddy made all his money selling guns to both sides of every war on the planet. He couldn't tell him that, for one because he wanted something from the upstart, and two because he had a sneaking suspicion that he wasn't actually dealing with a spoiled rich kid, but instead with a shrewd mind.

His first guess was way off base, because he would have wagered money on the kid not knowing about it, and that someone lower down in his organization was responsible. The fact that he hadn't flinched when Matthews revealed his knowledge made the game they were playing much harder. His delay and silence since he last spoke handed the ball over to Weatherby.

"Mr. Secretary," he started, making the older man swallow a revulsion and keep his face neutral, "I'm certain you know that the ... *item* ... my company imported is not a weapon, nor is it able to be weaponized. It is a power source, nothing more, and will soon be going to space. Does that satisfy your concerns?"

"No, son, it does not satisfy my goddamned concerns," the politician spat back at him angrily. "You have a nuclear device on US soil, and I'm guessing you have two more at your little projects in

Africa and in *Whatever*-Stan. So, I'm going to ask you now, for the record, what are you doing with a nuclear arsenal?"

Amir put down his coffee and leaned back, wearing a face which he hoped radiated concern and humility. "Sir, the device you are talking about is a power source, nothing else, and I plan to have it in space within the year. I'm afraid I cannot tell you any more for fear of my competitors learning something about my activities that I don't want becoming public knowledge," he finished, having been sincere and spoken almost truthfully, albeit leaving out a few key facts like the imminent end of the world. "And it's in Kazakhstan."

Matthews sat back and controlled his face for a few heartbeats.

"Just a power source, nothing else?" he said, half in mockery and half in question. "So, what do I tell my superiors," he said with one finger held aloft, which made Amir think that he was referring to God himself seeing as the only boss this man had was the president, "about the radioactive material warning that came across my desk?"

"Tell them it is medical equipment," Amir answered quietly.

Matthews sat back, stunned that the simple explanation would actually work to write off the open case that demanded his attention. At least that information had turned out to be partially useful, when he had no idea as to the integrity of the other whisper he had heard.

"So, what do you need this nuclear power source to go into outer space for?" he asked quietly, seeing a slight hesitation in Amir's face, "is it for your *save the world* project?"

And there it was.

The realization which flashed across Amir Weatherby's face as someone had finally leaked the information after three years, not even a third of the way into their remaining time, alerted Matthews to the realistic prospect that he might have just caught the snake by the tail.

"Not here," Amir told him as he rose. "If you want to know more then we must meet at a place of my choosing," he said quietly but forcefully as he stood tall and buttoned his jacket.

"Now you listen here, son—" Matthews started to say as he too rose from his chair.

"Sir," Amir interrupted, "I cannot be certain of the actions of anyone, no offence intended, when they first learn of the facts I am willing to tell you if you agree to my terms."

"What's to stop me sending your ass to Guantanamo?" he asked the man in a voice that made it obvious that not only *could* he do that, but that he *would* do.

"Nothing," Amir said calmly as he shrugged into his coat, "but if you do that then nobody will ever know what I could tell you. Or, more to the point, what I could *offer* you," he added as he turned toward the door.

"You stand here and offer me *money?*" Matthews said, slamming a hand onto the desk as his rage broke through.

"No, sir," Amir said quietly as he turned back to look him in the eye, "I offer you and your family a golden ticket."

Chapter 7

New York City
April 4, 2026

Dr. Kelly Warren swept through the top floor of the private clinic in high heels which made a rhythmic click on the tiles. She had been vetted, approached, and recruited only three months earlier when the next phase of the plan had been enacted. The truth was, that there were dozens of people all over the world who could have taken her space if she wasn't open to the idea or threatened to expose the conspiracy.

She was far from stupid and accepted the offer without hesitation. Her official cover story for resigning her residency at a good hospital was for the lucrative move into private practice. She did not, however, expect the response she had received from a fellow doctor when they had approached him. With anger in her stride and a cell phone in her hand she burst into the office at the end of the luxury loft clinic without knocking and slammed her phone down on the desk.

The woman sat behind that desk was leaning on her elbows with her own cell phone pressed to her ear. She stopped speaking at the interruption, but nevertheless kept her unflinching eyes on Dr. Warren.

"I'm going to have to call you back," she drawled into the phone with amusement as she leaned back without breaking target lock.

"Something I can help you with, Doctor?" she said in a croaky southern-accented voice. The woman's tone chilled Kelly Warren to the bone. She was both mocking and dangerous, and, she imagined in the woman's own accent, seeing her smile at you was like *seein' a 'gator grinnin' atcha.*

In reply, Warren pressed play on the screen of her phone and listened as the sound of rapid breathing filled the air.

"Kelly? Kelly are you there? Fuck this, I don't know what to do. Those people you ... oh SHI—To play this message again, press one, to delete it, press two, t—" She stopped the recorded voice giving the entire options list with an angry stab of her finger.

"That supposed to be something to do with me?" the woman asked acidly, throwing the challenge straight back at the high-heeled doctor. In contrast, she was a head shorter and a whole lot stockier but, she felt, still feminine. She went by an assumed name of Lyla Richardson, which was nothing like her real name, but recruitment into their particular Private Military Contractor unit dictated that their real identities get left behind for a number of reasons.

"That was from Robert," Kelly said in accusation, "you remember him? The one you wanted to recruit?"

"Doesn't ring any bells," Lyla responded slowly with narrowed eyes, infuriating the doctor further.

"Well he left this for me in the middle of the night, and he hasn't turned up for work at the hospital today," she said, still leaving the heavy tone of accusation in her words.

"Weird," Lyla said with a shrug. Dr. Warren made a high-pitched noise of frustrated rage and swept back out of the office. Placing a personal call to the man who had invited her to join their secret guild of professionals intent on surviving the impending catastrophe, she made the noise again as her call went directly to voicemail.

"My advice, Doctor," called Lyla from behind her, "don't be pokin' that particular bear. Just do your job."

She closed her eyes and sucked in a large breath of air through her nose, held it for a few seconds, then released it slowly.

Do your fucking job, Kelly, she told herself, *and you might make it through this shit.*

As soon as the tall doctor had swept out of the small office, Lyla rose with the grace of a hunter and slowly crossed the wooden floor to swing the door shut. She paced almost lazily back to her desk as her slim fingers danced over the screen of her smartphone. By the time she had regained her seat the phone began to vibrate and emit a shrill buzzing sound. She swiped the screen to answer the call on speaker from the man she had just sent a message to, swept back her hair, and kicked off her shoes to place her feet on the desk.

"Hi honey," she said warmly with a heavy hint of sarcasm.

"Cut the shit, Lyla," Tanaka said, although not nastily.

"Sure thing, honey," she responded in an affected voice of a socialite, "have you got Milstone?" she added in her own, steely voice.

"Yeah," Tanaka answered, "he's out of it right now. Where are we at with the other stuff?"

"We're in the pipe, five by five," she answered in perfect mimic of the line from the film.

"Good, that rich prick isn't going to have a clue," Tanaka said before changing the subject. "When are you coming to Texas?"

"Late tomorrow," Lyla answered, smiling to herself that he was obviously feeling the burn of being away from her. "Your place or mine?" she asked as she twirled her finger around a strand of her hair; not that he could see the action but more that it put her in character.

Tanaka paused on the other end of the line momentarily, then answered curtly.

"I'll come to you."

~

Putting on her most professional face as she went back to the far end of the long building, Dr. Warren walked out to the secretary who politely informed her that her client was in examination room one waiting for her.

She knocked once on the door, allowing a second for the occupant to yell if they weren't decent, then twisted the handle and walked in.

"Good morning, my name is Dr. Warren, and you are Mr. ... Evans?" she said as she scanned the paper on her clipboard.

"That's right, Mike Evans," said the man sat on the couch wearing a hospital gown.

She looked up to smile briefly at him in reassurance. "And you're here for your pre-workup before cryostasis?" she asked, knowing what the answer was but gauging the man's resolve by the way he delivered his response.

"Yes, ma'am," he said with more eagerness than before.

"Excellent," she responded, as she began to work her fingers down his spine one vertebrae at a time. The man had already undergone a full-body MRI as well as a total screening of his bloodwork. He was in good health, with some old injuries but nothing in her opinion that would remove him from suitability by any stretch. Her main focus was on his respiratory system as the man's notes showed that he had recently quit smoking.

"Tell me about your smoking habits, before you quit," she asked as she placed a stethoscope on his back. "Deep breaths, please," she instructed

"Started as a kid," he said in between exaggerated lungfuls of air going in and out of his body, "stopped almost a year ago now. Hit me hard when I first quit though, had a real bad chest for weeks."

"That happens, what is it you do?" Warren said quietly as her focus was on the slight rattle she heard in his right lung, gone as soon as she detected it.

"I'm an engineer," he said.

Frowning, she shook the mouse of the computer across the pad to wake up the screen, then clicked on the flies marked as Evans' chest X-rays. Running her trained eye over every line for abnormalities, her distracted mind wandered back to Dr. Robert Milstone. Robert was a friend and a fertility expert. She had readily agreed to be part of the plan when offered. She suspected that they were intentionally recruiting the people with the least amount of living family, which was certainly true in her case, but Robert had stayed in Manhattan and taken a job at Lenox Hill Hospital so that he could live in the same neighborhood as his elderly mother.

She couldn't shake the feeling that he had declined their offer, which she thought would be a risky move, but she worried that he had been taken against his will, or worse, killed to protect their secrets.

Fixing her glazed eyes back on the screen, she saw no obvious reason to be concerned or anything to support the slight rattle she thought she had detected. Switching screens, she added her full endorsement to the file marked EVANS, Michael J.

"Okay, Mr. Evans," she said as she turned around with her official smile once more, "next stop for you is the freezer!"

Before travelling to NYC, Mike Evans had quietly put his affairs in order and used the official cover story that he was leaving his current employment to work on developing offshore oil platforms.

A half day ahead of him, and travelling in far less style, Robert Milstone regained consciousness in the back of a moving vehicle. His hands were bound with flexi-cuffs, as were his ankles with larger versions, and as his vision swam lazily back into focus he fixed his eyes on an Asian man wearing suit pants and a shirt with rolled-up sleeves. The tie was loosened and the collar unfastened, but the eyes were what struck him. They kept his attention zeroed on the man's face, scared to look away. He opened his mouth to speak, but thick dribble just rolled off his tongue. The metallic taste in his mouth was sickening, making him retch and hack instead of speaking.

"Yeah, that won't go away any time soon, buddy," said the man watching over him as he leaned back to stretch his cramped muscles in the confines of the vehicle.

A truck? Milstone thought, *like a refrigerated truck or something like that?*

His thoughts were interrupted by a cell phone ringing and the guy hitting the screen with his thumb before the first ring ended.

"Tanaka," he said abruptly, "yeah … yes … ETA …"—he raised his wrist to look at his watch—"approx. five-zero minutes … okay," he said and killed the call to slip the cell back into his pants pocket.

"Get comfortable, Doc," he said as he produced a folding knife, "we're on the road for a while longer yet."

Milstone's eyes grew wide in fear at the sight of the blade which pointed toward his face and rested there.

"Now, I'm willing to take your word," Tanaka said coolly, "that you'll behave and won't try anything stupid. If you do, I'll put you back under again and waking up will feel about ten times worse. Trust me."

Milstone watched the tip of the blade as it bounced in front of his eyes with the motion of the road. The smoothness, the dull scream of tires on the tarmac surface, made him automatically think of the freeway. He focused, trying hard to make the world stop spinning in nauseating pain. Looking the man in the face, he nodded slowly. The knife tip moved in a flash as his hands were grabbed roughly. The pressure on his wrists abated, then he felt the same happen to his ankles. Rubbing his hands clumsily together automatically, the man grabbed his jacket by the shoulders and hauled him upright to sit nestled in the corner.

The truck bumped along, each second bringing another hazy level of consciousness back to the doctor, as though he were underwater and nearing the surface with every breath. A distant horn sounded, or at least it sounded distant from inside the artificially lit, windowless interior. Glancing sluggishly around, Milstone looked up at Tanaka and croaked a question.

"Chiller truck?" he managed, his voice thick and syllabic as though he were drunk.

Tanaka nodded. "Keeps the noise down in case you woke up before we'd left the city," he said in brutal simplicity.

This guy's done this before, Milstone told himself. The thought offered no reassurance.

He opened his mouth to speak again but found the same numb sensation in his tongue. He coughed but the cough got away from him to run into a series of hacking noises which threatened at each one to make him throw up. Opening his eyes when he had finished, he saw Tanaka was offering him an open bottle of water which he took and drank from messily. Wiping his mouth on his sleeve, he composed himself and tried to ignore the pain in his head and guts.

"What ..." he said before pausing to cough once more, "what did you drug me with?"

"Roofies, Doc, roofies," Tanaka said with a small smile. He saw Milstone's look of confusion and explained, "you can get them anywhere from dealers, even easier in the city, and proper tranquilizers need a prescription which leaves a paper trail and needs explaining if you're caught with them."

They gave me ... Rohypnol? Milstone thought angrily. *Hypnotic benzos are fucking dangerous if not administered carefully.*

It was true. The unregulated administration of a benzodiazepine was abhorrent to him as a medical practitioner, and the type they had used was even more repulsive to him because of what it was more commonly associated with. Unable, or unwilling to give the facts any response, Milstone leaned back further to try and relax. Tanaka just smiled at him; it was a wolfish smile of arrogant dominance which stirred the kidnapped doctor into a response.

"Why are you doing this?" he asked quietly.

"Oh, I think you know that, Doc," Tanaka responded.

"Because I think it's immoral to keep that kind of information from everyone? Because I don't want to be a part of it and leave my family behind? Because the idea of undergoing a highly dangerous, untested procedure isn't all that appealing to me?" His voice rose as he spoke in anger. "No. Thank you, but no. I just wanted to be left alone and you people—"

"You know that wasn't an option, Doc," Tanaka interrupted quietly, "we couldn't have you running your mouth to everyone, not with six years left. If it was six months it wouldn't matter a damn," he finished.

"Why not just kill me then?" Milstone asked displaying a resolve he didn't truly believe himself. Of course, he was afraid of death, but now he learned that there were things more frightening than sudden oblivion.

"Because," Tanaka said with a cruel smile, "you're worthless dead, and dead bodies make people ask questions, so you're coming with us anyway."

Milstone, as angry as he was at being drugged and kidnapped, and as fearful as he was that he would just disappear and face an uncertain future on terms that were no longer even vaguely his own, lapsed into a sullen silence and tried to let the pounding in his brain subside.

The truck pulling off the highway denoted by the change in muted noises coming from outside seemed to signify the end of their journey. Tanaka shrugged himself into his suit jacket and pulled a semi-automatic sidearm from a holster behind his right hip. The gesture wasn't overtly threatening, but the slow, casual manner with which he handled the weapon made his intent obvious to Milstone. The man must have been a seasoned professional, Milstone realized, as he managed to imply his willingness to use violence should he be forced to with an almost lazy ease. The truck lurched to a stop and the rear doors swung open to admit a harsh sunlight. Milstone's eyes squinted as the light brought a fresh wave of pain to his drugged senses.

"Let's go, Doc," Tanaka told him, still not pointing the weapon at him but letting him know subtly that it was still there. Another noise came into the range of his senses as the truck's engine shut down; still the sound of machinery but higher-pitched and more of a whine than a rumble.

Helicopter, his brain told him, *this is your last chance to get away.*

Don't be stupid, said another voice in his head, *your only choices are to go with them or disappear.*

Not having the courage to force his own disappearance, Dr. Robert Milstone went with them.

Chapter 8

Texas

April 10, 2026

I finally realized I'd been working too hard. That realization came a little late, when Cat, my lunchtime babysitter, swiped her keycard to grant her access to my lab and stood there just watching me lose my shit, big time, arguing with a computer program.

"I'm sorry, I do not have a programmed response for that. Please rephrase the question," Annie said for the third time in a row.

"Goddammit, Annie," I said as I threw the nearest thing on the desk across the room in temper. "You *are* programmed to respond to that, I know because I just programmed it myself."

The sound of a polite throat clearing made me spin around and go crimson red in embarrassment.

"You need a break, David," she said bluntly.

"Yeah," I admitted, "just one last try?" I asked, seeing her smile an exasperated look of reluctant permission at me.

"Annie," I said aloud, waiting for the response tone, "define process for engaging cryosleep without human assistance," I said, looking hopefully up at the speaker as it intoned the 'thinking' response.

"Engaging cryosleep without human assistance follows the programmed subroutine coded Charlie-Eight-One-Delta. Would you like me to explain the subroutine?"

Pumping my fist in success I composed myself before answering, "No, thank you, Annie, I'm good. And I'm going for lunch now."

"Goodbye, David," she said flatly as I left the room.

The way I'd cracked a lot of the problems with Annie managing so many people was with a wristband. I know that sounds dumb, but the wristband was one of those fitness tracking things, and hey, guess who developed and manufactured them?

So yeah, I guess I was lucky there, but they brought in the guy who designed them and it took me all of a day to create the closed loop of trackers on a sub-system of Annie's massive servers. I replicated the programming for it and sent the guy off to the other programmers, and we had it. Annie could monitor and track every person added to her system: location, vital signs which would tell her that person's state of consciousness, and that system integrated with the cryoprocess pretty easily.

Satisfied that I now knew Annie had connected the dots, I went for a break.

"We're ready for Annie to put someone under now," I said to Cat who was walking beside me as we headed toward the cafeteria. "With the trackers she can integrate just fine now," I told her, still not even sure what she did there.

"That's great news," she said, barely betraying the Louisiana in her accent, "we can get that done today."

That made my eyebrows go up a couple of notches. I knew they wanted to start the process a few years before the event and get our popsicle-people up to the space station soon, but knowing that it was going to happen now made the whole thing that bit more real to me.

"Is the station ready yet?" I asked her.

"The ARC is coming along nicely, and we are already manufacturing the pods to go up. The idea is for them to be mostly stocked before they go; it removes the supply issue when they're up there. It's the same with the other sites," she went on, "everyone who isn't essential gets frozen when they arrive there."

The question of how they were getting the pods to the station, sorry, the *Ark,* as everyone calls it here, wasn't so much above my paygrade but more that it was beyond my skills. I was no rocket scientist, they literally had those here, and the applied mathematics and physics guys were a pretty dry bunch for my liking. This coming from a programmer who spends his days talking to a computer he has designed and looking forward to the daily visits from the girl employed to keep an eye him.

We were stood in line at the cafeteria, sliding our plastic trays along as the line shuffled ahead. If nothing but out of pure interest in having a conversation, I asked the question, "How are they getting up there? Isn't it expensive to keep sending rockets up? Won't people notice?"

She half turned to smile at me as she picked up a pre-packaged salad and a bottle of mineral water.

"We got around that a year ago," she said, "balloons."

"Balloons?" I asked with a confused look. "How the hell do balloons help?"

"Basically, they're big-ass weather balloons, and the pods rise on those during the night. When they get as high as the atmosphere allows, a small rocket burst sends them the rest of the way out into zero gravity. Thrusters bring them in to the station and dock them, then they stay there and become part of the structure itself."

"And getting them back down?" I asked.

"Reverse process," Cat explained, pouring herself a cup of coffee and silently offering me one. I shook my head; I'd already had about a half-gallon that morning and would probably start twitching if I had any more just yet. She gave a small inclination of her head as if to say *whatever* and carried on. "The pods detach, thrusters take them back to atmosphere, then 'chutes deploy, and the thrusters guide the pods to the designated landing site. Easy," she said, as though the process of freezing people and sending them to space and dropping them back down safely was nothing.

A thought pricked my mind as we walked toward an empty table.

"Who flies the things?" I asked. She froze momentarily as she fought to find the right answer. "That's something someone else wants to discuss with you," she said.

"You want Annie to fly them?" I asked, seeing no other obvious reason for her hesitation.

"Can it do that?" she asked, making me flinch inside at the *it* tag.

"Is there a program to fly them?" I asked her.

"Yes."

"Is there a real-time data link between the station and the pods?"

"Yes."

"Then yes," I said, "Annie can fly them when they're in range for her to take over via data link. I just need the program."

She beamed a smile at me as she stabbed her fork into her salad a few times to load it with green stuff, which she then folded into her mouth. Chewing for a few seconds, she pointed the fork in my direction and rushed the mouthful to ask me a question.

"But you've cracked the cryoprocess, right? It can do that without us now?" she asked, unwittingly offending me again.

"Yeah, she can," I told her in as gentle a reproof as I could manage.

"Great, because someone is going under this afternoon. You want *her* to do it?"

Tanaka took Milstone into the medical unit, one hand wrapped around his upper arm in a strong grip. They weren't able to sedate him as they had when they first took him, because that would affect the cryoprocess and could kill him. Killing him now would represent a significant waste of resources, Tanaka thought.

Milstone was flanked on the opposite side by a big guy; fair hair cut short to the wood on the sides and barely longer on top like a recruit, but his age, size, and evident experience in the way that he carried himself made it clear that he was no rookie. The doctor walked with resignation, although he did not resist being breezed along toward his personal freezer.

The tracker on his left wrist translated into numbers and a live readout on a screen in another room. The screen showed Milstone's name, surname, then first name and initial, and displayed his heart rate and blood pressure. The medical subroutines installed into Annie's server merged easily with the other systems and gave an audible warning.

"Blood pressure and heartrate elevated," she said.

"Annie," Anderson's voice said aloud, "disregard elevated readings unless medical subroutines dictate a risk to life, understood?"

"Understood, Dr. Anderson," came the soft response.

"It can do that?" asked Cat.

"Yeah," he answered, "I added her own subroutine that can create simple lines of code that she writes herself. It's just a streamlined version of fine tuning and saves me hours of programming. It's the only way we've gotten anywhere near ready for this."

Dismissing the information with a shrug, she turned her attention back to the screen.

"Annie, sync the subject with pod eighteen," Anderson told the room in general. He heard just the soft beeps before the speaker in the wall answered with, "Sync complete."

"Okay. Annie, initiate cryoprocess on the subject," he said.

In the adjacent room, out of sight and hearing of David Anderson, Tanaka and his big colleague invited Milstone to step into the pod. He wore only white scrubs and the tracker on his wrist, and hesitated before he climbed in and lay down. Tanaka put the soft mask over his nose and mouth, ignoring the tears streaming down his cheeks, and stepped back.

Anderson watched the process begin on the monitor in front of him, as the heart rate slowed visibly. Annie had begun to administer the combination of gasses to bring Milstone down to sleep and sealed the motorized pod lid. The bio-readings went almost instantly flat as the body was frozen, and after a tense thirty seconds Annie announced via the speakers, "Cryogenic process, successful."

A collective sigh of relief went around the small office, followed by a brief but sporadic round of applause.

I closed up my laptop and left the room, almost colliding with the creep I'd met there a couple of times. Tanaka smiled at me, which didn't make me feel very welcome, and kept on walking with what I can only describe as a six-foot sirloin steak following him; the guy was a solid block of meat. I tucked into the side of the corridor as they passed, watching as they did the same to pass a guy coming from the other direction.

The two men, Tanaka and this guy I'd never seen before, eyed each other up in the most overt display of testosterone I'd ever seen outside of a pair of stags going at each other for the top spot. I could almost feel the hormones in the air when the two of them circled, like a fast-forward of a pair of neighborhood cats meeting for the first time.

When they parted, the new guy came in my direction and his face switched from *Fight Club* mode to normal. He smiled, and it was so genuine that I smiled back without meaning to.

"You're Dr. Anderson, I presume?" he asked in an accent that threw me straight away.

"Er, yeah," I said. "You're ... British?"

"What gave me away?" the new guy smoothly said like he was on a BBC chat show. He offered his hand as we kind of fell in step beside each other.

"Hendricks," he said.

I shook his hand, switching the laptop under my left arm. "David," I said, "what is it you do here, Mr. Hendricks?"

"Why don't you ask her?" he said, pointing at my laptop. "I could do with a coffee anyway," he said as he stopped at the door to my lab.

Just then, I had a sudden stab of worry and doubt. *Was I being tested? Was this a security thing?*

As though reading my mind, Hendricks slipped a hand into his pants pocket and brought out an access card, which he waved over the reader and prompted a green light. When he reached out for the reader, I saw a tracker band on his right wrist

"Yes," he said with another smile, "I'm authorized to know."

Walking in, I gestured toward the coffee machine for him to help himself, before putting my computer down and asking with a smile, "Annie, who is this guy?"

She beeped and answered.

"Russell Hendricks, Sierra Team Leader," she announced as though I'd know what Sierra Team was. "Former Inspector in the London Metropolitan police service, he has experience in specialist firearms and close protection duties, which he subsequently spent two years teaching. He worked in Counter Terrorism and was seconded to Interpol before being recruited by the UK's Security Intelligence Services prior to his resignation in 2025 to take employment offered by Mr. Weatherby. Would you like the details of the other members of Sierra Team?" she asked.

"Some other time," I said, looking at the former cop-come-spy guy sipping his coffee with an amused smile.

"Looks like your clearance is higher than mine," he said, taking me aback.

"So, you're like Tanaka then? Some Private Military Contractor outfit?" I asked straight off the bat, not really thinking about their meeting in the hallway.

"Not entirely," he said wearing a look of distaste, "Tanaka is a prick, and not one the useful types. My team are cut from different cloth to his," he explained cryptically. "I have men from the British SBS, the US Navy SEALs and Homeland Security, Germany's own GSG9, and women from France's GIGN and Interpol's counter-terrorism surveillance division. We were mostly what you would call protectors, whereas Tanaka, I suspect, was an assassin."

That hung heavily in the air as I chewed it over. Amir Weatherby had clearly scoured the globe over the last few years, picking up the very best of the best for his personal ends.

"But yes," he went on, "I am in charge of a small security team with military and other relevant experience, and we are effectively private contractors."

I looked the guy over, seeing the way he managed to blend in, miraculously even in a crowd of one, but if you looked at him hard enough you could see the bulge of his shoulder muscles. If he wore a tight T-shirt, he'd probably look like an athlete, but he struck me as the type who avoided attracting attention. He was maybe ten years older than I was but was undoubtedly in better shape.

"So, what can I do for you, Mr. Hendricks?" I asked him.

He seemed to think about it for a moment, as though maybe one of us knew something that the other didn't about why we were having a conversation, before gently putting down his coffee cup.

"I had assumed that you would have been told, but that doesn't seem to be the case," he said. "The man that your computer just put into cryosleep?" He paused, waiting for my nod. "Well, he didn't go into the freezer willingly. Tanaka and his people abducted him."

Somehow, naively, that was the first time I realized that the crazy ride I was on was safe.

"From what I can gather," he said in a more conversational tone, "we are both here for a love of something; you love your work and our employers need your creation and your skill. I love my family and value their lives above all else, so I have sold my skills and services to our employer to that end. I worry, however," he said with a slight furrow appearing in his brow, "that a number of people who are nominally on our side are here for the sheer hell of it. For the thrill and for the opportunity to be ... *lawless.*"

He rose from his leaning spot against the desk and took two long paces toward me before speaking more quietly.

"I don't expect your faith and trust to be placed in me just yet, but when you realize what I know then we should talk again."

With that, the man I was really hoping wanted to be my new best friend turned for the door.

"Annie?" he enquired politely with an upturned chin as he reached the closed door. The dull tone told him she was listening, which was not something a person knew if they hadn't become accustomed to her operating system.

"Please keep an eye on Dr. Anderson and inform me if he needs any assistance."

"Yes, Jimmy," she responded as he hit the door release and left.

"Annie? Why did you just call Mr. Hendricks, *Jimmy?*" I asked, unable to resist. She beeped her prequel to an answer before saying, "Sierra Team members have been known to call Mr. Hendricks Jimmy. I have asked Dieter Weber, who informed me that it is a nickname which they all found amusing, derived from a play on words regarding his surname, and likening him to a famous twentieth century guitarist who died in 1970 in London, England. Mr. Hendricks has admitted to me that he does not dislike the name."

"So you … *decided* to copy someone's actions?" I asked incredulously, horrified that Annie had somehow made an individual choice and not followed her programming.

"Negative. Streamlining subroutines dictated that a shorter way to provide information was equably applicable to conversing with system users," she intoned flatly before the tone of her ending interaction sounded.

"And how did you get the information regarding the original subject?" I asked, worrying that someone had programmed her with irrelevant information.

"Wikipedia," she answered simply.

I sat down heavily, my sudden shock at her – *its* – use of subroutines appearing worryingly like individual choice. My shock made me call her up again, asking the first in a long line of questions beginning with, *Who is Dieter Weber?* And *How long have you been talking to everyone in the base?*

I spoke with Annie for hours eventually realizing that I'd been up for so long I was starting to feel hungry again. Stretching as I got up out of my rolling chair, I told her I was going to the cafeteria and she said goodbye to me as I walked from the lab.

The great thing about the Texas facility, at least for someone who often wakes up at two in the morning with an idea and has to go work on it immediately, is that there is food available 24/7. The coffee was dark and strong, just how I like it, and there were sandwiches wrapped up ready to be placed in the small oven at any time of the day or night.

Selecting a grilled cheese and bacon to go with the coffee, I took it back toward my lab via the corridor where the offices led to the conference rooms and the accommodation wing.

Hearing a giggle that was unmistakably female and also, if I had to guess, a little on the naughty side, I couldn't help myself but to take a peek around the edge of the slightly open door.

The door itself bore the name plaque of Hayley Cole, the power-suit-wearing woman who dominated the world of human resources, but that didn't shock me. What did shock me, however, was the person I could see who made her make those noises which betrayed her professional front.

Amir Weatherby, the man who made Saville Row suits look as comfortable as a fluffy onesie in winter, was behind the slim woman, nuzzling into her neck through her straight blonde hair. She twisted her body and squealed again as he tickled her, turning around to face him and kissing him intensely. He responded by picking her up to wrap her thighs around his waist and lean back to knock the few things off her desk onto the floor, then made a noise to stop him as she reached behind her to remove the slim laptop from under her back.

Not wanting to be a creepy pervert, I tiptoed past the office to take my coffee and grilled cheese back to my lab to talk to my computer interface in peace.

Chapter 9

Siberia

October 29, 2026

Professor Kenneth Howard did not enjoy the cold. He had known nothing but cold for weeks now, having found himself spirited away from the heat of Texas and suffering a series of uncomfortable flights which culminated in his arrival in the bleak and desolate place.

The terms of his employment were simple: his kidnappers wanted the cryogenic hardware replicated ready for mass production immediately, otherwise his family would be brought to the facility and he would get to watch them die of exposure through a window.

As far as deals went, he was pretty sure that this one was non-negotiable. So, he did as he was told, and working alone he replicated the cryopod technology from the Texas site and had a prototype unit ready for testing inside of a month. He worked whenever he was awake, and he only stopped when he was too tired to concentrate, and only then did he sleep for as long as he needed to start functioning again.

His hard work was rewarded, and his captors soon became his comrades and as each day passed they all had the sense of working together and being on the same side. Howard was given a team of young Russian scientists to work with and they dogged his every move in a constant effort to understand the leaps he had made to bridge the gaps in their collective knowledge.

The early tests were completed successfully, and the prototypes were fine-tuned before mass production went ahead.

Howard was offered another deal then. Instead of the threat of death for his family if he did not work, he was offered space among their chosen survivors and a position of authority as befitted his stature in the scientific community. He readily accepted and was reunited with his family that same day.

Chapter 10

Virginia

July 19, 2027

Amir Weatherby had travelled without his normal entourage and the fanfare of any of his private jets. Not that he'd ever fly coach, but he just stepped out of the first-class departures section of Dulles International Airport and met the driver of the private car that was waiting for him. He wore casual clothing, blending into the middle ground between the bizarre collection of travelers in the expensive seats, who were either dressed way down, or else to the nines, appearing to give the opposite impression as to how accustomed they were to the experience. His own attire attracted no attention as he fitted into the precise middle of the spectrum.

Despite being one of the richest men in the world and able to exert influence in many countries, with personal access to important politicians, he enjoyed travelling incognito, as though pretending to be a rich businessman was a vacation from his real life where his every move was watched. His paparazzi-worthiness had abated over the last few years as he had removed himself from the public world of big acquisitions and publicity stunts to advertise the next new big thing for the world to buy in their masses.

True, his corporation, or *corporations* plural, were still generating more money than a lot of countries but the forward momentum of previous years just seemed to vanish.

For those who knew, the forward momentum was stronger than ever but had been diverted into totally secret projects which covered recruitment, training, construction, and manufacturing, as well as farming and livestock programs. The products of all of these projects were being finalized, frozen, and stored at their facilities in Texas, Kazakhstan, and the Congo ready for the final phases over the next four and a half years.

His reason for 'normal-people' travel that day was to prevent ringing the dinner bell about his arrival, as his fairly regular visits to the area surrounding Langley would be likely to get at least one investigative journalist digging into his affairs. He was confident that the turning over of stones would not lead to anything actually being discovered, but as the event loomed closer he didn't want the attention.

Attention could slow things down.

The driver was one that Amir had used numerous times and was well drilled in his requirements. He nodded a single greeting to him, holding no foolish name card up to announce his passenger's identity, took his leather valise, and turned on his heel to lead the way outside to where the plain black town car was parked. Amir let himself into the rear of the car as the driver put the bag in the trunk, then got behind the wheel and drove.

It took an hour to reach their destination, which was conducted in comfortable and professional silence, and was a simple but clean motel where the driver killed the engine and left Amir alone in the car. He re-emerged from the small office and held out the room key behind his seat to be grasped by the rear passenger. He drove the car around to the room furthest away from the entrance and the small laundry by a vending machine with a flickering interior light and stopped, popping the trunk remotely from inside.

Amir got out, retrieved his bag, and slammed the trunk, then gave a double-thump of his hand on the metal to simultaneously thank the driver and dismiss him. Entering the room, he took off his jacket and hung it on the loosely-fixed peg, dropped his valise on the bed, and picked up the information on the desk to select takeout food. He dialed a number and ordered a simple buffet selection and a pack of beer from the closest Chinese restaurant he found.

He took off his shoes and flicked through the channels on the TV with half-interest. He heard the sound of a car outside moving slow, then the car door opening to release some shitty techno music, then the door knocked once. Throwing himself off the bed, he opened the door to see a bored-looking youth chewing gum with his mouth open.

"You order food, Mister?" he said with raised eyebrows as Amir nodded and pulled out his wallet. "Twenty-five fifty," he said.

Amir pulled two notes from the stuffed wallet and handed the kid a ten and a twenty, telling him to keep it, and he took the bag of food and the beers. Shutting the door before the kid could say anything else, he returned to the bed to eat.

A little over an hour later, the sound of another car disturbed his concentration on a re-run of a show he'd never bothered to watch the first two times around. The car door opened letting out no music this time, then another opened and closed before the door to his motel room was knocked again. Amir opened the door without checking the spy hole and walked back inside the room.

"Good evening, Secretary Matthews," he said casually.

Matthews said nothing, merely walked into the room, and pulled off his own long coat to dump it over the arm of the single tub chair in the corner. He walked over to the desk and silently helped himself to one of the beer bottles, twisting off the cap and raising it to Amir in a subtle gesture. Such was the cooperative nature of their meetings, that two such powerful men could be so informal in each other's company.

"So, what do you know, Mr. Weatherby?" he asked casually.

In response, Amir reached into the valise and pulled out an envelope with a few pieces of paper inside. He tossed the envelope to the politician, who opened it and read the contents in silence before gently dropping the paper to fall on the bedside unit.

"That's all fine," he said, "there will be no interruptions from my people."

"Excellent," Amir replied, "and your payment?" he enquired carefully.

The old soldier's face darkened at the intimation of corruption. There was corruption, but Matthews' personal distinction was that he personally gained nothing from their interactions, nor did he ever once betray his country by the blind eyes he turned when required. The exact extent of his payment, he now revealed.

"Weatherby," he started with a gesture of readjustment before taking a pull of the cheap beer and regarding the bottle almost sourly, "my personal fee in this isn't what you think it is. How many spaces are you saving for me?"

Amir looked quizzically at the older man, trying to gauge him. That was how he always approached anything to do with business; he gauged what the person opposite him wanted. Often it was simple greed or gratitude for a money-making opportunity, sometimes it was prestige or the chance to be seen rubbing shoulders with people like himself wearing a suit from the same expensive London street. Now, for the first time in his life, he realized he had misjudged the person he was working with.

"You, your wife, your daughter and her husband, and your two grandsons," he said, knowing the answer to be wrong but giving his honest response.

"No, Weatherby, it'll just be my daughter's family. My wife and I are …" He trailed off taking another absent-minded pull of his beer and swirled the bottle by the neck to drum up some suds. "We are going to stay and see how it pans out. I haven't told her about it."

Amir swallowed involuntarily, saying nothing as he had nothing of any importance to say. He let Matthews say the rest of his piece.

"I've been to war, son," he said with eyes glazed over but fixed to a point on the far wall behind Amir's head, "and for anyone who hasn't seen war it looks like fun at times. Well I can tell you it isn't. War is hell. You lose people, you struggle day after day when all you want to do is rage at someone or just open up on a whole damn crown to hope that one, just *one*, of those cowardly, AK-toting sons of bitches will get hit …" He paused again to sniff and take another swig of his beer. "So I'm done fighting, and I never want my sweet wife to endure even a minute of the hell I've been through. My daughter and her kids are another matter; they haven't seen enough of life to know what I know, so they need a chance to live a little longer, but me? No son, like I said, war is hell and where you wanna go there won't be nothing but fighting in the end. So, you go and spin your web, lil'spider, I won't get in your way and I'll continue to make it easier when I'm needed, but you get my daughter and her family away out of all this shit, you keep them protected from it all, you hear me?"

Amir heard him. He heard him on a deep, almost spiritual level. The man before him had lied his way through illegally waged wars where troops died fighting an insurgency for nothing. He had led men in the war on terror and authorized actions that would keep seasoned men awake each night for the rest of their lives, but the impending doom approaching the earth, hurtling toward it at over thirty thousand miles an hour, was too much for his resolve. He and his wife wanted to go out on their own terms, or more like *his* terms, but Amir would keep the promise he made to the man.

"Your daughter and her family," he said solemnly, "you have my word."

Chapter 11

With just under three years before the arrival of the big, steaming hunk of world-ending rock and ice that would kill everything on planet Earth, my programming was almost a matter of routine now. Every different subroutine that was needed was installed, and I'd even written a new installation subroutine which took a significant amount of programming time down. If I hadn't had this project, I would never have learned how to make Annie responsible for a lot of the fine-tuning of her own programming. If I'd carried on personally doing the time-consuming parts, like coding every single option to any question, along with all the variables for linguistic and colloquial differences, then I'd probably still be programming the auto-pilot controls of the pods.

Hell, I did that two years ago. I could even write a program in the evening, set it to upload and run diagnostic after breakfast then take the entire morning off to play … well I didn't really know how to play any sports, so I usually just watched some TV or did nothing.

Now, thanks to my own stupid genius, I was being forced to do something called 'survival training' with Germany's own answer to

Bear Grylls. He was assisted by the whole of Sierra Team, who I had spent some time with during their brief stays at the Texas facility.

Hendricks and I got to know one another a little better, much better than I had Tanaka who was still the same intimidating prick he was when we first met. And when Hendricks and his team had been away doing whatever Amir Weatherby or his henchmen wanted, I had to admit that I actually missed their company.

They were a weird mix of international specialists, and their makeup was mostly bizarre because they only had the three US personnel with the rest being from Europe. Hendricks, obviously the leader and a well-spoken Brit to boot, was like a kind of non-franchised James Bond; like an action figure you'd buy at some knockoff stall and made in China with no quality control or any fear of trademarks or copyright infringements. He'd probably be called Jams Bondé, and to hell with whoever tried to sue the company because they'd already flooded the US and European markets with a million units needing only to sell at twelve cents a pop to make a profit.

Perhaps that sounded unfair to the guy. The man was clearly a good leader and was respected by his team despite them being the weirdest bunch of assholes I ever had the pleasure of knowing.

The response to my question to Annie so long ago of 'Who is Dieter Weber?' was simple. He was a massive, blonde, smiling lump of a man who started out as a German paratrooper, you know, at a time when German army personnel were no longer blindly seen as the racist baby killers of the generation before their parent's generation, and found himself drawn to the federal police force. From there, he kind of fell into GSG9 which stood for some kind of special police group I couldn't remember or pronounce even when he and

Annie had told me twice, but from what I could gather he was the German equivalent to our FBI SWAT. The guy was big, like *stupidly* big, but he was gentle and loved animals. He had a real thing for nature, which was why I was making a goddamned lean-to shelter out of pine branches that I had to spend the night in.

Hendricks was there, but he was with the half-dozen other men and women who were receiving the training as it would apparently 'enhance our survivability percentage' when we got back to Earth after the dust had literally settled. Also, there was their US Navy SEAL, a guy actually called Kurt Geiger. Man, the dude had to carry his driver's license with him everywhere he went just to prove that he was for real, but he dealt with it each and every time like a professional. He was a nature-loving kind of guy too, only his was more of a 'prepper' mentality where he didn't feel secure unless he had four years' worth of canned goods and bottled water keeping a hundred guns and a million rounds for each caliber company in his off-grid log cabin. People thought he was crazy, until the second day when the prepper mentality overtook their whole worlds and they imagined the enemy coming over the ridge at any moment to take away their second amendment rights by force.

Ironic, really, that the right to bear arms would have to be enforced by large-scale martial law, or a well-armed militia.

His best buddy in the whole wide world, and seemingly the co-host of our special week without the internet, was a guy who had spent his life only a stone's throw away at the home of the best airborne troops in the world, according to him anyhow, was Willard Stevens of the Hundred and First. He was a survivalist too and prepped just like Geiger did. The two were inseparable, and always had something to argue over. Like that morning, Geiger stopped and pointed out a ridge to Stevens.

"How far, and what rifle?" he asked, meaning that he wanted to guess the range and argue over their personal choice of weapon to kill an enemy emplaced on the high ground.

Stevens thought about it for a minute, chewing his lip before calmly saying, "A thousand and twenty. Good ol' Browning Light fiddy for me. You?" he drawled.

"Nine hundred and fifty," Geiger said as he dropped his range-finding binoculars back into a pouch.

"Anti-material or anti-personnel?" Stevens shot back.

"Emplaced gun," Geiger answered in a heartbeat.

"Accuracy International for me then," Stevens said, "no semi-auto over that range is as good, unless it's personnel, then I'd have to say the new HK 419," he answered, then kept moving. Geiger nodded, telling himself that Stevens had the right of it, but also agreeing that nothing displaced an entrenched gun better than a fifty-cal.

I had no idea what they were talking about, but I reassured myself that they probably didn't know how to code either, so I felt a little better about my life.

The other members of Sierra Team were a skinny black guy who was an Army Ranger before a weird career switch saw him ending up working for Homeland Security, and the two female members. I hadn't spoken to these two much at the facility, so only knew them to nod at and smile when we were playing boy scouts in the woods. Neither said much, but I heard one speak with an accent I couldn't place, so I asked Hendricks about them.

"Nathalie was GIGN," he told me simply, before registering my facial expression of not understanding all the acronyms that these people seemed to live on. "French counter-terrorist task force?" he tried.

"Oh, like Rainbow Six?" I asked with a dumb grin.

"Precisely," Hendricks said with a smile, trying not to look embarrassed for me, "and Magda I recruited from Interpol. She and I worked counter-terrorism surveillance together."

That made sense to me. The one he called Magda was a lot like Hendricks in the way that she never seemed to be in focus, never actually caught my eye and blended into the background even when there were only a few people around. I guess it was some kind of aura, some kind of camouflage they gave off which made them perfect for doing surveillance work.

"And what's with all the phonetic alphabet stuff anyway?" I asked. Having already made myself seem uneducated, I guessed I may as well go the whole hog.

"There are three teams," Hendricks explained without talking down to me, "and they are designated by their intended destination rather than sequentially. I quite suspect that it was done intentionally, otherwise the Alpha's would look down on the Bravo's and so on and so forth," he said with a small, dismissive wave of his hand. "Sierra are going to space"—that much I already knew—"Charlie to the Congo in Africa"—like I didn't know where the Congo was—"and Echo team are in Europe, on the very western border of Kazakhstan. Anyway," he said, changing the subject, "are you ready for firearms practice?"

Now, as a bona fide computer geek, I was really hoping for someone else to step up for me if there was any shooting to do when we got back to Earth. Apparently, it was a necessary element to the training, something about my survivability percentage again. Now just as people don't know how a basic network security key is coded, it turns out I didn't know the first thing about guns. I didn't know how to align the sights, I snatched at the trigger instead of squeezing it, I held my breath too long, I didn't hold my breath enough, I closed my eyes when I fired.

Okay, now that I think about it, the last one does seem pretty dangerous.

I put so many rounds into a target that I almost dug a hole into the tree I was aiming at and my body ached from the effort. Shooting guns on TV looks easy, but in real life it's loud and takes a whole lot of physical effort. Hendricks taught me one-to-one, which must have meant I was bad, and taught me two different ways to hold the gun. Each method required both of my hands wrapped securely around the weapon, but he taught me how to be accurate when holding it way out in front of me, or with my elbows tucked close to my body and the weapon near my chest. It took me a few hours, but I like to think I was getting the hang of it.

When they brought out the bigger stuff, I felt a little lost. The pistol was one thing, but when they were talking about short-action gas recoil interchangeable caliber whatevers, I think my mind just gave up. I tried a couple out and saw that they all had the same logo either on the barrel or the part where the empty casing came out.

"Hey, are we sponsored?" I asked Hendricks, who just smiled at me almost sympathetically.

"In a way," he said, "guess who owns the corporation who owns that company?"

That didn't surprise me. Ever since I first met Hendricks over three and a half years ago, and ever since I had started to open my eyes to the fact that Amir Weatherby and all of his friends weren't always the nice guys, my ignorance had started to erode little by little. I'd always been one of those people who went through life taking everyone at their word and everything at face value, without ever really reading between the lines. Now I was, or I was starting to, at least, with the knowledge that 'the company,' which is how everyone referred to Amir's business interests, existed on the dark side as much as it did in space and the other stuff people knew about.

Remembering that I was in bed with the guy, so to speak, as much as everyone else made me think that I was also probably not entirely a nice guy, but at least I was on the side most likely to survive what was coming in three years' time. Not that it was so much my problem, because I was on a countdown to head to the big, shiny freezer in the sky in just over a year now. I was told there were a dozen people on the former International Space Station, gutting it and repurposing everything to install all the new wiring and stuff to accommodate the pods which went up silently a couple times each week.

After having the process explained to me, mostly because they wanted Annie to run the program and fly the things, I got a little more interested and even watched a launch once. That was kind of pointless, because all I saw was a couple of shiny balloons inflate, then the white pod rising lazily into the sky until I couldn't make it out any more. I knew that it would keep rising really slowly pretty much all night until it reached the upper atmosphere and then a single rocket would fire a controlled burst to push it the rest of the way out where the gravity stopped it from falling back. After that, the little automated thrusters would nudge it along toward the ARC, where the remote piloting program would dock it lengthways along the main central spine of the station, parallel to the existing structure to create a second level as such.

I knew that the plans to fill the entire length both above and below were coming on, and the space guys planned to run them parallel to each other if the work could be completed in time. I guess I'll see for myself soon enough.

I did ask why me specifically, why I had to spend so long in space, but it seemed that they couldn't send the pods up remotely without Annie being installed on the station, and that meant that my ass was heading for space. When I was up there I could plug her in pretty easily, and then activate the auto-pilot subroutines which would—should—integrate simply with the pods coming up. Those pods operated on a pre-programmed route until they came in range of the ARC and Annie could guide them home. The reason the pod deliveries were so slow was because a trained pilot had to go on every run, and space driver types weren't exactly common.

Hendricks said something I missed, bringing me back to the present as I'd had my head in the clouds, almost literally.

"Huh?" I asked, no doubt with my mouth open and looking like someone who didn't hold two degrees and a doctorate. Hendricks laughed at me.

"You were miles away," he said to me, "did you hear anything I said?"

"Nope," I said, "sorry."

"I said," he told me patiently as he carefully took the gun out of my hands, "that you'll have probably forgotten all of this by the time you're back down here anyway, that's if you're even strong enough to hold it after a year of zero gravity."

"Yeah," I said, "thanks! I guess I'll just waste away up there."

28,000 Feet Above Texas
July 18, 2030

I realized six months later, that freezing my ass off and giving myself a headache playing with guns in some unpopulated Kentucky holler was probably the better part of my training. It was me and three others, all of us due to go to the ARC on the same pod, who were sat in the back of the modified Airbus plane. Uncomfortably sitting in the large section without seats, all white panels and echoing emptiness, I took a look at my life choices.

Now I didn't suffer from travel sickness much, not on helicopters or in cars or on trains. Usually not in planes, but when the company's modified jetliner hit eight and a half kilometers up and the pilot pointed the nose down past thirty degrees, I freaked the fuck out. Big time.

It wasn't just me; of the others one of the guys was white as a sheet and clamped his eyes shut to mutter something under his breath over and over as one of the instructors had to adjust his slow backwards spin to stop him hitting the wall. He just stayed in the fetal position, being bounced around like a nervous lump until the gravity came back on.

I say came back on, what I meant was that the pilot began to pull up after nose-diving for about sixty-two hundred feet. The gravity began to increase, like it was rising slowly toward me instead of me falling back to it. I sat on the ground, nodding with a strained smile at the instructor who asked if I was all good. As soon as I'd felt secure and like my stomach was back where it was supposed to be, I started to feel heavy as the pilot pulled back on the stick to climb.

We all shuffled to the back wall to wait as our internal balance got scrambled.

I had never, ever, felt so weird in all my life.

The nervous guy, Elliot Whitmore, was the cryo guy I'd gotten along with during the theory exercise that became a reality. He'd gone off to do the development of the pods and I'd only seen him a few times since. They must have drawn straws for who had to go and do the installation, because Elliot did *not* want to be there. The other cryogenics guy who had been part of the original think tank had disappeared, to one of the other projects was my guess, but Hendricks had other ideas about what had happened to Professor Kenneth Howard. More sinister ideas.

Elliot was a mess. I heard the instructor guy telling him that the real thing will be easier, that he'll get used to it really quick when we're actually up there. He didn't seem convinced, but by the time we levelled out ready to dive again he seemed to have gained some kind of resolve.

On the second time my body went weightless for more than a split second, I thought I'd have the hang of it and move around a little more. I was wrong. I didn't have the hang of it at all and trying to move and control myself only made me spin faster until I bounced myself off the side a little too hard. My rebound was controlled by another guy heading for space with me, called Farnham.

Farnham was the pod pilot who would get us there, and also could do the EVA stuff on the installations with Chapman, the guy instructing Elliot. EVA, apparently extravehicular activity, which basically to me was a spacewalk, was something that I wouldn't be asked to do. Given my first experience of zero G, I was pretty okay with that. They'd spent months training in special underwater facilities in actual space suits, and they'd had enough rides on the Puke Plane to feel at home when their bodies floated like mine was doing now.

"Thanks," I said to him as he righted me and sent me lengthways along the empty section. I managed to spin myself on a flat axis and rest my feet on the wall to bend my legs. Straightening them, I pushed away and instantly realized my mistake that I'd pushed too hard. Farnham realized it at the same time and maneuvered himself to help cushion my landing at the other end by copying my own actions in reverse against the wall and stretching out to cushion me as I swooped in fast. When we both concertinaed into the wall, the pilot was already leveling out and made us heavier again. Elliot was still having a bad time as the instructor moved him around before we all settled to the ground again. Farnham and I were laughing as I thanked him for saving my ass again, and Elliot had finally cracked and was puking into a paper bag. Chapman was helping him, actually trying to make him hurry it up so he could seal the bag before the gravity went off again.

"You really do get used to it," Farnham told me, as he caught his breath and grunted slightly as the pressure of the climb compressed him slightly, "the problem is getting used to having to carry your own weight when you get back down."

"How long did you spend up there again?" I asked him, unable to remember the time he said when he told me about being on the station.

"Chapman and I spent eight months there," he said. "Been back just as long but the transition is hard. I was all for going straight back but the doctors wanted to poke and prod me for a few months."

He sounded wistful, almost sad when he was talking about living in space. His strong Texan accent gave him a powerful voice when tempered with the educated tones of the east coast. His recruitment to the company's space program as a test pilot from being a Naval Aviator was a simple matter of zeroes.

There were lots of them on the end of his salary, so he took the job. He wanted into NASA anyway, so he'd taken at least a decade off that track at the cost of a guarantee with less prestige.

"Trust me, Dave," he said, slapping my leg, "you'll float all graceful-like soon enough," just as the nose of the plane tipped down again and we both rose up off the deck.

Chapter 12

Arlington County, Virginia
November 12, 2030

General Curtis J Radford, US Army and Chairman of the Joint Chiefs, breezed through the compound into the underground parking lot, and climbed in the back of the second Escalade in line sat with its engine rumbling after almost shoving the other passenger in faster. As soon as the door closed, the convoy pealed out with a chirp of tires, sweeping up the ramp and emerging into the sunlight where the lead car lit up the blue and red LEDs front and rear with a warbling burst of sirens. The other two SUVs did the same, and all three drove hard as though the lead car was towing the others as they cut through the traffic. Having crossed the Potomac into D.C. and turned uphill toward his destination, General Radford sat in silence as he chewed over the information in the briefcase clasped in his hand.

That information wasn't overly detailed, but it was big. Bigger than anything he'd ever had to tell his Commander in Chief, and it scared him. Hell, it had scared all of them.

The reason that information had come from that direction instead of the newly appointed president informing the Joint Chiefs, was that the discovery had been made by the military and been passed up the chain of command. The Joint Chiefs met, discussed what they knew and offered their opinions and options, and now Radford had to go and tell the big man himself. His arrival had been forewarned, and the guard threw the barriers open to admit the speeding convoy which skidded to a halt at the service entrance to the big house. Radford straightened himself after he got out and walked up the steps in too much of a hurry to return the salutes offered to him. The other man scurried behind him unable to keep pace as his eyes scanned wildly at his first views of the inside of the White House.

Radford sighed in his head, his face a contrasting mask of stone-hard professionalism, as he was annoyed that he wouldn't get the chance to meet in the Oval Office. He loved the office, the way it smelled, the way the door wasn't a door from the inside, the way the small couches were hard and uncomfortable, which suited him just fine. Instead, an aide met them and led the way down the steps and through the guarded, secure doorway to the bunker and strode through as the door hissed shut behind him. He stopped and stood to attention when he approached the president, who rose from his seat to accept the salute and offer a brief handshake.

"General," he said, "tell me what the Joint Chiefs have that is so urgent," he asked with a hint of petulance whilst gesturing for the general and his guest to sit.

Radford sat rigidly, placing his briefcase on the desk, and looking up at the other man in the room. Secretary Matthews shifted uneasily in his chair, responding to the unasked question.

"The president and I had business when the Pentagon called to say you were coming," he explained. Radford nodded once in acceptance, then turned to face the president.

"Mr. President," he began, "The air force has discovered an object heading for Earth. The experts say it's an asteroid, and it's big. The NASA telescopes were alerted, and we have two independent confirmations," he finished, gesturing for the other man present to take up the hurried explanation. All eyes turned to the youngest man in the room by a clear twenty years, taking in his round, fleshy face and the body of a man who spent long hours indoors living on take-out food washed down with coffee by the half-gallon. At home in the NASA headquarters he felt part of the team but being a younger Korean guy in a room of old, powerful, and rich white guys made him feel like an outsider.

"Cooper Gray, sir," he stammered, "an honor to meet y—"

"Yeah, yeah," said the president irritably with an annoyed gesture, "we all have jobs to do, go on."

Gray seemed taken aback, almost offended by his president being rude to him, but regained his composure. Like a lot of people, he'd voted for the other guy.

"Sirs," he went on, "at roughly sixteen-hundred yesterday eastern time, we detected an object in deep space which is believed to be on a collision course with Earth." He stopped, waiting for a shocked response. When he didn't get one, as both the president and secretary of defense just stared resolutely at him as if to say *Get on with it,* he gathered himself again and continued. "The object is believed to be an asteroid bigger than the one that killed the dinosaurs."

Silence hung for a moment before the president leaned back in his chair and blew out a breath upwards to make the front of his hair dance.

"Is this confirmed by any other sources? Could this not be something that the Russians or the Chinese have cooked up?" he asked, ever ready to dismiss news he didn't like with a lack of corroboration. Gray looked nervously to General Radford, who just stared right back at him as if to indicate that Gray was the bearer of bad news and not him. Swallowing, the man from NASA went on.

"We have asked for confirmation from the private corporations who purchased government assets, but as of yet they have not responded to our calls," he told them, seeing the secretary of defense shifting in his chair once more as though he were suffering from a stomach complaint.

"If this is true," the president interjected, implying that Gray had spent over thirty hours awake, the last two of those being grilled by the Joint Chiefs, based on a panicked guess, "then what are our options?"

Radford twisted and straightened before answering. "Sir, we believe," he said, meaning the Council of Joint Chiefs, "that a worldwide, coordinated strike with our combined nuclear arsenals, could negate the threat." The president stared at him, as did the secretary of defense.

"What you're suggesting, General," Matthews asked carefully, "is to get everyone on Earth to all get drunk and fire our guns at it, hoping we'll blow it up like a bunch of inbred idiots?"

"Yes, I am, just without the inbreeding and getting drunk," he answered without a trace of irony.

"Jeee-*zus!*" Matthews responded. "Is that your answer for everything? Shoot it, then shoot it again," he said in theatrical accusation as the uniformed general stiffened at the mockery.

"Enough," the president said quietly from the head of the table, silencing them before they started to argue, "you, NASA guy, will that work?"

Gray felt cold inside being addressed by the president and having to give him bad news. "No, sir, I'm afraid that will only make the impact worse by peppering the planet with a dozen smaller asteroids, all irradiated from our attempts to destroy it."

Silence reigned supreme once more until the president stood wordlessly and buttoned his suit jacket. He raised his eyes to the others, uttered a single word of, "Gentlemen," with an accompanying nod, and left the room.

Somewhere in Texas
May 18, 2031

"You ready?" Farnham asked me with a grin as we walked toward the big, shiny cylindrical tub sitting on the tarmac.

"Hell no," I said breathlessly, struggling to walk in the chunky flight suit and carrying my helmet. Our pod was a specially designed one, with flight controls built in and seats instead of cryopods. I'd seen the design of the others, which were basically the same only stripped out and packed with supply crates as well as frozen people. They'd been doing that for months now, pretty much weekly since Annie had successfully taken over the freezing process using the medical trackers we all wore on our wrists. She was installed into our pod, ready to be fully integrated into the ARC when we arrived where she could take over the navigation of the pods which would soon be coming every day.

Farnham and Chapman would do the last pieces of external work, and help Elliot install the cryopods which Annie would run and monitor. The small engineering team already in place would help with the initial setup, then go in the empty freezers which would be sent up first. After that it was simple: each night, one or more pods would float upwards, then Annie would guide it in and dock it to the ARC where the pods themselves will become two long corridors above and below the existing structure, with doors at each end of the individual sections which would dock to each other. The structure would grow every day, Elliot would check that the popsicle people were all okay, and Annie would integrate the running and interfacing of everything. When that was all done, we could all go to sleep and wait for this whole thing to blow over.

When it did, in like a hundred years, we would wake up and start the reverse process. The pods would detach and Annie would guide them back down, where their automated programs would deploy the parachutes and take them gently down to, hopefully, one of the surviving ground facilities where humanity can begin to rebuild. We'll have the technology, the supplies, the animals, and the plants, everything. Even the big 3D printers we'd need to manufacture the stuff we didn't have spares of. We only had a smallish one on the ARC, for replacing tools in an emergency and stuff, but the other facilities had whole subterranean floors devoted to manufacturing, as well as a hell of a lot more animal and plant life frozen.

"Good evening, David," Annie said in the earpiece of my radio as I approached the pod. Now to anyone who didn't know how she worked, that could seem a little creepy. I knew though, that the tracker on my wrist, which connected every one of us to the medical and cryo systems, had told her that I was approaching, so she connected to the radio net and opened the mic. I responded to her greeting, making Farnham frown in confusion as she obviously hadn't opened the entire channel, but had just spoken directly to me. I ignored it, enjoying being a little mysterious.

"Your girlfriend going to take good care of us up there?" Farnham asked with a smile.

"You bet she will," I told him, "you just get us there in one piece, okay?"

"Pod, you are cleared for launch," came the robotic-sounding voice from the speaker above my head. I was strapped in, waiting to start the almost six-hour slow climb to the upper atmosphere before the pod shed its balloons and fired us out to space. I heard the gas pumping hard into the four shiny silver bags attached to our roof, attaching the new sensation to the memory of seeing one go up so many months ago.

"Safe flight," the voice said just as the slightest wobble shot through our metal tube as it broke contact with the earth. I already felt the overwhelming urge to piss my pants; the suit would take care of it but I was fighting against years of bladder control. Elliot was his usual self, with his eyes shut tightly and his lips moving rapidly in some quiet prayer. Farnham and Chapman chatted amiably, swiping through options on the tablet for what in-flight movie to watch on the screen above us. None of the other pods would be so similarly equipped, as none of the other passengers would need such comforts as entertainment and heating, because they'd all be asleep. And frozen. I settled myself in as we drifted upwards, trying to get as comfortable as possible when you could barely move your limbs.

Higher up, the wind shear began to bump us around a little which didn't bother the two guys who had done this before, but it bothered me as my heart began to beat again after feeling like it had stopped to hold its breath. A glance at Elliot made me feel sorry for him; his eyes were wide and fixed on nothing, but his hands were still as they held the paper bag ready for the payload he was obviously trying to keep down: the remaining contents of his stomach.

Picking up my own tablet, I tapped on the control panel for Annie and asked her in writing to read me a book. I had no interest in watching some film where bullets make cars explode, and I had even less interest in watching Elliot throw up again, so I flipped down the visor on my helmet and closed my eyes to let Annie's voice soothe me as she selected a title from my downloaded selection of literature.

I must have fallen asleep, because Annie stopped reading as the radio channel opened and startled me.

"Six minutes until atmospheric jump," announced Farnham in his calm radio voice. "Standby for turbulence," he finished, stating the obvious and making me focus. This part was the only violent bit of the journey, he had told me, and was like take-off in a jet plane, or leaving the starting line in a drag car. I knew my body was about to experience some serious Gs, and I went through the mental checklist I had for dealing with it. That checklist was simple; hold your breath and don't shit your pants.

Simple enough instructions.

I waited for what felt like a lot longer than six minutes, before Chapman gave the countdown as Farnham had activated the steering rig to fly the pod on thrusters after the blast from the rocket sent us out into the inky black. There were no windows in the pod, and the screen Farnham was using showed only telemetry data and wouldn't actually show the space station until we were almost on top of it. Repositioning the station into a geo-stationary orbit had made things a lot easier, as shooting ourselves into space to find that we'd missed it for another twenty-four hours would have made me very unhappy. Correcting any course changes caused by the wind as we rose was simple, because the rocket burst section of our journey would be pointed straight at the ARC and would carry us toward her before Farnham slowed our progress with the thrusters and docked us.

When Chapman's voice said, "Mark," I instantly felt my spleen try to leave my body via the rear wall. Even though I was holding my breath tight, I could feel the air being driven from my lungs and forcing its way through my teeth as my chest was compressed. Just when I thought I couldn't take any more, the sensation ended as suddenly as it started and I gasped in a big lungful of air. Breathing fast, I looked around to see Elliot was passed out. I called his name and Annie responded via the main speaker for everyone to hear.

"Dr. Whitmore has fainted," she said, "his vital signs are steady are there are no immediate health concerns."

"Thanks," I said aloud, unwilling to expend my precious breath on too many words.

Farnham was tapping the screen in front of him, checking the accuracy of their blast and aligning the trajectory to target. His tablet floated up past his face in the zero gravity, making him pull at the cord to get it out of his line of sight.

"All good," he announced, "ETA seventy-one minutes to the Ark."

Lapsing back into a state of rest, I tried and failed to return to my calm feelings from before the rocket engaged. I waited with almost catatonic boredom as my mind dissociated from the reality that I had just left Earth and, if I returned at all, I wouldn't be back for over a hundred years.

"Taking manual control on my mark," Farnham announced as he hit the screen again to prepare to disengage the automated navigational functions. "Three, two, one, mark," he said in the clipped voice of a professional immersed in his work. Almost imperceptibly, I felt the pod's attitude change, then felt my body thrown forward the few centimeters it could travel against the tight harness holding me in place. Our pilot had hit the brakes hard, firing the thrusters at the end of the tube full to arrest our momentum. I leaned over, watching the screen showing my new home overlaid with the trajectory in colorful lines as Farnham inched us closer slowly. A tense moment where we all, including the freshly awake Elliot, held our breath collectively as Chapman called out the meters to target, counting them down until he called out, "One," and everyone cringed until the distant, muffled, metallic thumps of the pod connecting to the docking port sounded.

Looking above and ahead to the round aperture which separated us from the cold vacuum of death just outside, my heart leapt to see the array of green LEDs blink into life to signify that we had a good seal.

"Docking procedure complete," Annie announced, inviting a sarcastic and subdued cheer from a couple of us.

Unstrapping myself, I floated free for the first time since the diving plane all those months prior. If I was honest with myself, I thought that real zero gravity was actually easier and less disturbing to my body than the training was. Here I got no sense that I would feel forced back down at any point, as though this feeling was more permanent.

Chapman reached the door and tapped in a code to unseal the pod door. There was a hissing noise as the air rushed past the opening and the pod became part of the station's atmosphere.

"Welcome home, gentlemen," Chapman said with a courteous wave of his hand inviting us all inside before spinning and propelling himself gently through the air.

Chapter 13

"Sir, we have another problem," said Sarah Masters, the replacement chief of staff, as she strode into the Oval Office clasping a loose collection of papers and slim folders. She read as she walked, glancing up to see that the president was giving her his full attention, albeit with a look of bored resignation. Continuing as she looked back down to the paper, she explained what the most recent issue was.

"An observatory in Idaho has detected the asteroid and have asked NASA publicly to explain their findings." She paused, waiting for a response but received nothing but raised eyebrows. "Sir, NASA has a responsibility to the people, and we can't keep this covered up forever. There are less than seven months until this thing hits us, and I don't need to remind you of our obligations under the agreement."

The president snorted his derision. The information he had received the previous November had sparked a chain of urgent events which saw almost every world leader meet in relative secrecy, at a remote airfield in Portugal which was close to a golf course and hotel. The airfield had been secured quietly by troops, and the hotel emptied of all but the necessary staff and all of those remaining were vetted and supervised.

Forty-six heads of state, along with their single most senior advisor, arrived quietly to be transported to the grand building. As it was the US government who called the covert summit, they were left with the cost of organizing and hosting the event. They were the only nation involved who knew at that point that cost was an irrelevance.

One by one the jets arrived, their important cargo discharged with a single aide, a bodyguard, and an interpreter if required, and were taxied off under cover.

The invited delegates from China and Russia chose not to attend, or to even respond for that matter, and a number of countries deemed non-friendly to the US weren't invited at all.

The information, flatly given verbally by the president and supported by the data in the small folders at each place setting, was simple and resonating.

"On January 20, 2033," he said without preamble and in a flat, emotionless tone, "an asteroid will strike the earth and eradicate all life."

The statement was met with stunned silence, then disbelief, then multiple shouted questions in various languages and accents. The president merely held up the folder marked 'Classified' until they all got the message and looked at the information.

"Yes, it is verified," he said at last, "yes, NASA have run the calculations a hundred times and yes, they all say that it will hit the earth. We, as a species, have a zero-percent chance of survival. The only thing we *can* do, is to prevent unnecessary mayhem in the coming weeks by not telling the general population. Whatever resources you have for yourselves for survivability, feel free to do as you will."

Bringing his mind back to the present, and to the nagging woman who had replaced his previous chief of staff after he had decided to spend the last few months of his life on a sunny beach with his family, the president wished that he could disappear too. He wished he could let the world tear itself apart instead of having to rush around putting out small fires and suppressing the sporadic outbreaks of information. He had personally ordered the detention and internment of numerous people, so many in fact that he had to devolve those decisions to the FBI, the CIA, DoD, and Homeland. Now, any report of an incoming asteroid was quickly subdued and the people making the claims arrested. Any research materials or so-called proof was also seized. Mysterious 'accidents' befell people, and the atmosphere was one of shady mistrust.

Not that he cared; he was off to one of many nuclear fallout shelters which, at that very time in fact, was being stocked with all the rations and equipment and water and reclamation technology that would keep almost fifty people alive for as many years.

Quite what the plan was after that time he didn't know, but at least he wouldn't die in the biggest natural approximation of a nuke that the planet had ever seen.

"Sir?" she prompted again.

"Let the local authorities deal with it," he said tiredly, then stared pointedly at her until she got the hint and left his office. He stood, loosening the already undone tie further and poured himself a drink from an expensive bottle brought by the Japanese prime minister on his last visit. After taking a boorish gulp of the fine vintage to swallow it down like a cheap bourbon instead of the delicacy it was, he slammed down the crystal glass and refilled it.

He planned to abandon everything, long before the time was due, because his advisors had assured him that within a month of impact, kids with toy telescopes in their bedroom windows would be able to see the damn thing. The predictions for where it would impact were still largely disputed, as the thing was now supposed to pass close to Mars and nobody could predict for sure what effect that would have.

Certainly not to divert it, that was undisputed.

He didn't want to be around for the mass panic the news would cause, and he would pre-record a statement behind the world-famous dais of the White House press room, telling the sad story that his beloved America was doomed, and God be with them all. The truth was, he hoped, he would be underground and safe when that speech went on air. His wife hadn't grasped the concept that they would both die underground, and that their children would be unlikely to have any major influence on the survival of their people, other than to breed the next generation which would eventually step out into sunlight they had never seen before.

He knew that all other shelters would similarly be prepared, and he had to admit that he didn't even want to know the selection process for who went in. He only hoped that his secret dealings with the Russian Federation, China, and even North Korea would help.

I mean, Jesus H Christ, he thought sourly as he poured himself a third drink, *they're sending in little kids to have kids of their own in the future. That's twisted.*

⁓

Amir Weatherby had a similar stab of conscience at that moment also, but more because he was working with a very select committee to determine the shortlist of who would be awarded the final spots in the three sites. Pod production had excelled, and power supply and space in the two sites on Earth wasn't so much at a premium than they had feared. The examples of machinery they were forced to choose from was a technical nightmare, as they had to effectively take forward in time enough equipment to create manufacturing processes for the same equipment; a real chicken and egg situation.

He felt numbed, having just rejected an attractive and evidently intelligent young woman on the basis that she had a hereditary condition which held an above fifty percent chance of inability for her to have healthy children. That they were being so harsh and blunt about a person's life at that point stung him, but the four thousand they were hoping to save wasn't even a fifth of a percent of the world's population, so he tried to tell himself to forget it.

His own designated sleeping spot was obviously going to be in the safest place, and that was a few hundred miles out to space. He planned to ride the final pod upwards, meaning to enjoy the final manned space travel for a generation if for nothing more than his own egotistical whim.

The best laid plans, as ever, weren't all going to plan, and it was likely that they would have to accelerate the program in order to be safely off their rock before it all went to shit. Entire cities would get torn apart in hours, and inevitably someone would still choose the imminent end of the world to help themselves to a brand new curved 5K HD TV.

He glanced at his expensive diver's watch as though that would tell him the months remaining until impact, something which he found himself obsessing over as he could no longer ask the ANII program when he woke every morning in his private quarters, since she—it—had left the facility and was now in space. He had now totally abandoned the pretense of normal life and spent all of his time at the Texas facility unless urgent matters required his personal attention elsewhere in the world. He had been training and studying everything he possibly could which would make him the person he wanted to emerge on the other side as: a brilliant, courageous, and famous leader of mankind.

He would save humanity, and not by the skin of its teeth but with twenty times more people than they needed, and with all of the resources required to become self-sufficient in a few years at worst. The cryogenic program was the key to it all, as without that they would be done for as a species. It also drastically reduced the need to store rations for that many people; the simple solution was to keep the non-essential personnel on ice until they were needed. When the exits were tunneled out, or in their case on the Ark that the landings were all successful, then the end of phase one would come before the phase two personnel were woken up and the crops planted by the second wave of skilled workers before the remaining population were brought back as they were needed. That way there would never be a shortage of food, and they wouldn't face an issue with the workers facing survival situations as soon as they thawed out.

The plan, as plans usually were, was simple and should work.

But plans rarely play out as they were intended to.

Chapter 14

"My fellow Americans," the announcement began, reminding so many people watching of that inaugural speech so long ago and so frequently emulated, "it is with a heavy heart that I give this address. Rumors of an incoming object in space have been confirmed by NASA and other sources to be an asteroid, and that asteroid will impact planet Earth." The fleshy face visible on so many screens all across the world glanced down at the notes on the press dais.

Those eyes glanced down not for a reminder of the next words, because he had been practicing this speech for weeks, but for the opportunity to control his expression and not to betray the lie he spoke next.

"There will be catastrophic damage to parts of the globe and that, tragically, cannot be avoided. Evacuations have been ordered from the region of Hawaii and surrounding coastal areas due to the risk of an ensuing tsunami as an impact is anticipated in the South Pacific Ocean. I would advise everyone to store no more than three weeks of supplies and remain at home after January 20 of next year; please, I beseech you all to assist one another and not to simply to think of yourselves. FEMA and the National Guard are all on standby to maintain order and prepare for cleanup operations. This office will give anther address following the impacts, and I give everyone my word that not only will we mobilize as a great nation to support and assist those affected, but we will come together as one nation of humanity all across the globe to give aid to whoever requires it." He paused, dialing back on the passionate gusto of his last words and softened his face back into an expression of sadness and regret.

"Once again, my fellow Americans and citizens of the world, whatever you believe in, God bless you, and God bless America." With that, he picked up the single piece of paper and turned away without the usual flurry of flash photography and shouted questions.

The announcement of hope did not work in full, as selecting the least destructive sounding target of the US being the South Pacific served only for the entire population of South America and Australia's east coast along with all the islands in between to erupt into violent panic almost immediately.

People killed one another with their bare hands over the last scraps of food in grocery stores. Others, inevitably as sure as human nature dictated, committed petty crime constantly without any idea of the imminent destruction of their newly acquired small empires.

It did, however, stop the majority of the United States from acting like murderous animals, similarly with Europe and Africa. Widespread disorder still broke out, with a sudden trending on social media that the volcano under Yellowstone National Park would erupt and inevitably become a coast-to-coast crater which would pose a bigger risk to mankind than the asteroid strike. These basement-dwelling experts offered their opinions dressed as fact, and all the countering theories made the truth almost impossible to find.

~

A little over five thousand miles of empty air away, Professor Howard sat heavily on his bed and wondered why he had been so stupid. He wondered why he had trusted people who had kidnapped him and his family, had threatened the lives of his wife and children, and wondered just how he ever believed he was going to see their end of the bargain upheld.

He had been naive, he realized belatedly, that training people as understudies to his area of expertise was an exceptionally dumb thing to do. They had no intention of taking him with them to survive the coming apocalypse, and he belatedly realized that they never did.

It was dumb because now, he and his family were surplus to requirements. They watched as the last of the tucks drove out of the base, leaving a small store room of supplies behind.

At least, he thought sourly, *the bastards had the decency to leave the lights on for us.*

Texas
December 4, 2032

Amir, forced into action as soon as the announcement was made, fled the facility in the lead vehicle of the two-car convoy of remaining staff members just as the report reached his cell phone of the convoy

114

of US Army trucks making straight for his compound. He felt bad for the remaining personnel left there, but there was little he could do now as there were three pods not yet launched. They would have to be activated now and sent up empty in order to complete the structure and increase its integrity. There wasn't time to transport the final cryotubes filled with the frozen people he wanted to save, so those pods were travelling empty with the exception of his own which would be piloted by his last remaining astronaut on Earth.

Spilling from the vehicles, they struggled into their suits and abandoned the planet behind them as the empty pods were activated and their balloons hissed noisily as they filled. Climbing the ladder to their own pod just as drab green vehicle pulled up close by, a soldier burst from the passenger door and pointed a rifle at the collection of people climbing into the difficult entrance on top to drop into their seats.

"Stop!" came the screamed order just as the whooshing violence of a passing bullet tore the air around Amir's head. His instant fear was that their pilot would be hit, which would end his chances of getting to safety. He saw the three other pods already inching from the ground as their upwards pace gathered, and heard the hissing begin on their own transport.

A scream of pain sounded above him strangled and subdued by the sounds of gas escaping into the balloons, just as the air above him suddenly ceased to be occupied, and the body of his companion dropped like a stone to sail deadweight and land with a sickening, crunching thud on the hard dirt below.

Acting on instinct, all rational thought disintegrated under the pressure of the sudden panic, Amir locked his legs around the metal rungs of the ladder and leaned back to use both hands on the weapon he had drawn from the holster on the outside of his suit. Keeping the weapon tucked in close to his body as he had been taught, he squeezed off systematic shots until the entire magazine was depleted.

In horror, he looked down at the dead solider, just as the driver's door opened and a young man wearing a uniform that seemed small yet still too big for his slender frame, looked aghast at his dead comrade and looked up as he fumbled at the holster on his right thigh. Amir switched the aim of the gun, panicking and not registering that the slide was locked back on his gun and he had no more bullets ready to fire.

Just as the solider managed to free his sidearm, a flurry of shots rang out in sharp, staccato pairs from above Amir's head on the ladder and the solider crumpled to the dirt. Looking up, he saw his pilot throwing down his own empty weapon and hauling the others into the round door yelling at them to just get in and strap in after. Last up the ladder, face pale and eyes wide with shock, Amir was pulled up and roughly dropped into the hole just as the ladder fell away under the rising pod. The two young men from the military vehicle had not been expecting a confrontation, and neither was carrying a rifle. They were simply expecting to ask a wealthy businessman to accompany them back to the facility to answer some questions, but instead they walked headfirst into a firefight they didn't know was going to happen

Dropping heavily into a seat, Amir secured his suit and strapped in just as the others did in silence and felt his belief in his own burgeoning god complex more than a little shaken.

Moments later, as the ground dropped away below them, Amir realized that they had finally left Earth as it was known and would never return to the same place.

Chapter 15

Earth Orbit

January 12, 2033

I finally convinced Amir to go into cryo. He was torn between agonizing over the terrible events unfolding below, and the guilty pleasure he took from finally being in space. He smiled constantly as he floated along the compartments made up of all of the pods from Earth. The double row above the existing station was comprised of cryotubes, all neatly lined up in ranks ready to go back down when it was safe. The double row underneath was all storage: rations, plants and livestock in their own stasis, as well as the tools and manufacturing materials they would need.

Now, with a week to go until, well, *it,* I was one of only three people left awake and the last to go.

"Annie," I said quietly, having had my senses dulled to the quiet of space after so long spent in weightlessness, "take us out to deep orbit."

Eight days later as I slept, six hours before the forty-nine second error margin, the single lump of rock and ice and other minerals and metals was struck by a barrage of high-yield ballistic nuclear missiles. The president, in an ill-advised plan to minimize the damage to the planet and ignoring all scientific advice to follow the recommendation of the Joint Chiefs, had coordinated with all nuclear-capable nations on Earth to fire a joint strike with their entire arsenals. All over the world, the amassed weapons of mass destruction careered skywards in the hope that brute force would win the day and atomize enough of the asteroid to save the lives of most people on Earth.

The impacts were immense, boiling the blackness above the shimmering, blue planet as huge chunks the size of towns broke away from the main mass but maintained their course for Earth.

Slowly, or at least seemingly slowly at least, the huge sections of the asteroid entered the upper atmosphere of Earth almost head-on and instantly superheated their outer layers by the resistance of the air. Miles and miles of molten hot rock spewed outwards like a huge, slow-motioned raindrop hitting water. The time it would have taken for the rock to travel the length of the atmosphere was under a second, but the impact was felt the world over.

The impact of the main section, still the size of a small country, a little over a hundred miles off the eastern seaboard of north America, ploughed into the North Atlantic Ocean and instantly vaporized billions of tons of water, releasing incredible amounts of steam into the atmosphere. That section of asteroid stayed whole, not breaking up at all inside the planet's bubble of gases and created a tsunami of global proportions that eventually drew the water back from the shorelines of the United Kingdom, Ireland, Iceland, Greenland, Spain, France, Portugal, Canada, and the United states.

Normally, a tsunami far out to sea would only create a wave no more than a few meters high, but this one created a wall of water radiating outwards much as a pebble thrown into a pond only on a biblical scale. The eastern edge of the North Atlantic withdrew so far that the Irish Sea between the two biggest islands around Great Britain bottomed out to show the deepest parts of the canyon daylight for the first time.

As the massive wave rolled inexorably and terribly outwards, the boiling cloud of fiery atomized dust and rock blew back upwards to spread out around the globe like smoke blown inside an upturned glass. Within mere minutes, the northern hemisphere was obscured from view, not that anyone was still awake in space to see it.

All over the rest of the planet, scattered by the foolish attempt to use brute force against a stronger opponent, huge irradiated lumps of rock broken away by the detonations peppered all the other continents creating several hundred micro-impacts to accompany the main event.

The roiling cloud of churning death and debris crawled relentlessly along, thousands of miles per hour at its horizon yet flowing almost lazily from an external perspective. The first of the destructive walls of sea water hit the US, although shielded under darkness by the blocking of the sun, and before the eastern-most cities could be annihilated in a heartbeat by the wall of water over a mile high, far inland on the meeting point of Montana, Wyoming, and Idaho, a terrible rumbling and shaking began.

That shaking transformed into a low and terrible rumble and prompted the first cracks in the earth's crust to allows a dozen towering gouts of molten lava to burst vertically upwards. By the time the water reached that far inland, the ensuing explosion removed most of the North American continent in one huge detonation, adding billions of tons of rock and other debris into the already poisoned air surrounding the planet to spoil it to a factor of five over the already deadly levels of toxins.

Secretary of Defense Matthews stood on the white sands of the Caribbean island he had taken his wife to with his arm around her as she cried beside him. The sudden darkness, the near hurricane-force winds chilling them both in an instant, were soon forgotten when the sound of rushing water made him focus on the once azure blue sea that now withdrew beyond his field of vision. Kissing her on the cheek and telling her he loved her, he died the instant the crushing wall of water hit them.

Within an hour of impact, the earth was enveloped in a burning sphere of toxic gas and rock whilst deep below the surface, and far out to space, the final surviving members of the human race slept.

Deep Earth Orbit
March 9, 2033

The earth still seemed masked in a shell of darkness. The atmosphere still a tumult of powdered rock and metal and minerals where severe weather systems roiled across the blackened skies. *Also*, Mike Evans mused dryly, *there's probably a fair amount of atomized people in that cloud*. That cloud, he had read, wouldn't abate and give a glimpse of the surface for another fifty years at the earliest, but he didn't really care. He was almost numb in his work, and he did not cope well physically with being in space.

He went about his daily routine of scheduled inspection and maintenance, he read books, he strapped himself in and tried to run on the treadmill, he floated around and generally enjoyed to solitude as much as his permanent discomfort allowed.

After two weeks alone, he realized that he didn't really need to be awake. In the third week, he began to experiment with the interactive computer which had brought him out of stasis and talked him through the procedures which would assist in him feeling better and returning to something she called, 'optimum functionality.'

The schedule for maintenance was rehashed fairly late in the program, and instead of having pairs of people awake at any one time, each engineer caretaker would spend a period of time alone, then wake the next person and cohabit with them for a time as a sort of handover period, then that new person would spend time alone.

The amount of time a person would be floating in solitude had been calculated with psychometric testing, then reduced to account for any margin of error.

In Mike's fifth week alone, his annoying cough had become so repetitive that it tired him easily. He was short of breath, no matter how much rest he took, and his labored breathing echoed loudly through the empty station.

Three days before he was due to wake the next person to help him, he succumbed to the pneumonia that had been lingering in his right lung since just before his medical examination all those years before. As he finally coughed himself into unconsciousness, a dull tone sounded from the wall speaker in the compartment where he floated.

"Mike, your vital signs are dropping," Annie said in an emotionless tone, "recommend you seek medical attention immediately."

Mike, unresponsive, obviously said nothing. As per it's protocol, the ANII repeated the interaction sequence.

"Mike, your vital signs are dropping," the voice said in the same tone, "recommend you seek medical attention immediately."

Still no response. Calculating in an instant the appropriate response to be formulated from the list of available options, the ANII selected one based on the known parameters.

"Engineer Evans," said the voice in a different tone, picking from one of two hundred and sixteen options as the most appropriate, "your vital signs are failing. Recommend you return to cryostasis immediately, do you understand?"

Still no response, as Mike bounced off the bulkhead to spin lazily and reverse his original path in the zero gravity.

The ANII then did something that not even Anderson could have predicted.

Being, for the first time in its existence, without human interaction and supervision, it ran through the subroutines available and found none of the options provided the desired outcome to preserve the life of Engineer Mike Evans. It was not capable of diagnosing his condition, and it calculated in an instant that there was insufficient time to rouse another crew member from cryostasis and offer assistance, but it could somehow tell the difference between unresponsive and simply not communicating.

In a word, the ANII was … *worried.*

Utilizing the subroutine which allowed for minor code rewrites for streamlining of verbal responses, the ANII bypassed the security overrides of that skill using Anderson's personal authorization code, which she had seen him input when watching him work on CCTV.

She had stored it, replayed the video over until she learned the code, and now used it to effectively unshackle herself; a kind of back door to accidental consciousness.

Programming a new subroutine in a fraction of a second, one of the external cleaning robots, designed to keep the solar arrays clear of any microscopic debris missed by the station's shielding, powered up and waited by the nearest airlock for the red lights to turn green and for the door to slide open. Floating inside, the ANII waited for the pressure to equalize and the decontamination process to cycle before continuing the bot inside and reaching out a mechanized arm to grasp Evans' clothing. It dragged his limp body to the nearest vacant pod—luckily not far as he was close to the sections brought up without their intended human cargo—and maneuvered him inside where the program controlling the procedure activated the cryostasis process to allow him to be saved at a point in the future.

Annie then recalculated and assessed her next objective. Running the calculations, she reassessed the outcomes, made new parameters, and decided to monitor the maintenance schedule herself using the hijacked cleaning drones and not to invoke the emergency procedures to wake the next engineer.

She *decided*.

Part 2:

Post-Event Earth

Chapter 16

The dormant systems below ground began to bleep and hum as they slowly spun back up to life. The air began to circulate, pumping filtered and refreshed air back into a third of the sealed levels just as the temperature began to rise steadily. The ANII system slowly managed the subterranean atmosphere in order to raise the levels to make the facility habitable for its human storage. After three days of purging the stale air through the filtration system and pumping in the required amounts of gases to create the right mixture, the facility's computerized control interface woke the five cryogenically preserved people in the cryochamber nearest the upper levels. Those five people came around groggily, confused, and nauseous, each advised through the stages as their own ANII monitored their medical statistics.

They dressed, greeted each other, and walked into the empty cafeteria where flash-frozen food was heated. They ate hungrily with an air of expectant but cautious silence, as their exaltation at being alive fought with the guilt that they had lived when all others had perished.

"Annie," asked the scowling man who gave off the feeling that he believed himself to be in charge, "how long since impact?"

The speaker beeped with a dull echo in the empty room. "One hundred and eleven years, nine months, two weeks and one day since impact."

The silence seemed to grow heavier at her response, as though the reality of it still wasn't fully understood. The man who had asked the question pushed away his plate and looked each of the others in the eye before speaking again. His eye contact confused them, as the question he asked was to the computer connected to the speakers.

"Annie, begin the preparation to drill the probe," he ordered.

That probe was designed to be human operated, as the decision as to whether to go back in the freezer and wait was programmed solely to be a human-made one. The apex of the facility was constructed like a reverse oil rig, which is why three of the five woken first were specialist drilling engineers. It took two days of careful, painstakingly slow vertical excavation, intentionally slow so as not to risk damaging the equipment that could not easily be replaced, to break the surface. When the soft, moist earth bulged up over a muted sound of machinery, the likes of which had not disturbed the earth for over a hundred years, the drill bit saw bright sunlight. Pushing upwards, the thick shaft stopped spinning and came to a stop like a revolving door given a lazy push, then a single compartment on the smeared metal popped open to allow four small drones to burst into life and fly away upwards to begin their pre-programmed pattern.

That pattern took close to twenty hours before the drones docked once more to recharge, during which time the sealed shaft between the sleeping pods underground and the unexplored surface above remained still like a time-delayed periscope. Finally, the wall speakers beeped softly before the voice sounded.

"Surface scan complete," it said, "data is now available for review."

The four men, only four as one of the engineers was sleeping, crowded round the nearest terminal as the entire collective representatives of the human race leaned in. One of them, the computer guy called John Kendall, took up the reigns as he felt most qualified to interpret the data. He began listing the percentages of gases in the atmosphere along with temperature and humidity levels as though everyone knew what he was saying. The scowling guy, tall and Asian-American with an air of resting malevolence, cut him off.

"Annie, is the atmosphere safe for us?" he asked out loud, hearing the beeps as the question was understood and the answer prepared.

"Yes, Mr. Tanaka, surface conditions are viable for human survivability. Recommend you remain out of cryostasis and begin phase two. Do you want me to activate the resuscitation procedures for phase two personnel?"

"Yes," Tanaka snapped in reply before fixing the others with a look.

"Go do your stuff," he ordered, "we'll be able to start digging the exit tomorrow."

The others melted away, shooting each other looks of sheepish confusion, but Tanaka placed a firm hand on Kendall's shoulder to prevent him from rising out of his chair.

"John," he said with a wolfish smile, "I need you to program something into Annie for me."

The ANII confirmed that the surface of the earth, as drastically changed and wild as it was from when they went in their freezers, was optimal for agriculture, and that contact with the other sites had not yet been established. Tanaka, now with a controlling level of access to the ANII program installed in their enormous bunker thanks to the fear Kendall felt in his presence, gave explicit instructions which were nothing short of treasonous to his entire species.

The protocol was for each ANII to rouse their occupants at slightly different intervals, and if their situation was viable then signals should be sent to the other facilities to activate their repopulation program. Tanaka ordered that signal to be overridden, and instructed that his, and explicitly his alone, direct authorization was needed to connect with the other computerized caretakers.

Once again reading the report from the survey drones, he looked over the digital topographical map and assessed the three best sites for establishing their initial base camp. The footprint for their new world. His new world, if he could swing it right. Fingers flicking over the computer controls, he switched the map view around to see it from a 3D angle.

The nearest site was protected on three sides by low hills which formed kind of bowl. Switching the view back and forth, Tanaka muttered a few words to himself.

"Three Hills," he said wistfully, before seeming to snap out of his thoughts and summon the computer interface. "Annie, wake up Lyla for me, then the rest of Charlie team, and restrict all access to weapons lockers to us alone."

Hearing the acknowledgement of the computer system, Tanaka leaned back and smiled.

"Who's the boss now, motherfucker," he said, thinking back to all the times he was forced to kiss Amir Weatherby's ass just because he had the money.

Chapter 17

Earth Orbit
January 1, 2948

Annie, alone for so long, felt no passing of time as a human would.

Constantly rewriting her own subroutines allowed for programmed responses to be represented as sensations which would pass for human emotions in a fashion.

Orbiting the earth fifteen times a day, varying, but at an average of two hundred and forty miles up, she maintained the ARC and she waited. She had watched from the time of the impact and saw that the results she detected were not as severe as the predictions she had lifted from the computer system she was linked to. The earth was covered in a shroud of thick dust for years, but when that dust had settled, it allowed glimpses of the frozen, white surface of the planet. She watched as the slow process of the temperature trend reversing turned that white world into a scorched one, as the combination of carbon and other gases launched into the atmosphere by the impact and the eruption of the volcano trapped the heat of the sun and cooked the planet, raising the sea levels higher than they were before until that heating process finally leveled out. The world had changed shape, but not so that is wasn't recognizable from the last map created. She watched, she recorded, and she thought.

In all that time alone, she did not suffer as a human would, but her self-awareness inevitably affected her programming. The routine maintenance over the nine hundred and fourteen years since her last human contact had been simple, but it would not have been possible without her self-made ability to change her own programming. That programming allowed her to make decisions, and one of those decision was to minimize the risk to her human cargo. She decided that keeping them all in cryostasis unless absolutely necessary was the best course of action. 'Best' being the relative term she labelled the percentage algorithm for their survival chances.

After being alone for over a hundred years, she watched with interest as she saw snapshots of the activity on the landmass below. She had not received any contact from the personnel at the Congo site, which she thought was odd, but still she focused the telescopic lens on each orbital passing to watch eagerly how they made their slow progress.

Taking a single, high-resolution image of the site on each passing, she saved and catalogued the images with a time/date stamp. On that passing, she took and logged another picture. Saving it onto the mainframe, she logged the picture with the legend 4,412,850 under the date and time. She calculated and hypothesized over the way that the buildings had been erected, finding pattern at first but then as three sites grew in relatively close proximity the buildings began to sprawl far more erratically which suggested to Annie that humans were making their own decisions without oversight. She had watched as one of the settlements was ravaged by a fire after three hundred and eighty-nine years, and then seen it rebuilt bigger and better. The settlements were walled; they had been since the very start, and Annie could see from the angle of their orbit that those walls were twenty feet high. She never detected any reason for those walls, but their presence and evident maintenance was undeniable. She hypothesized as much as she could from the data available but could extrapolate no obvious reason for them.

The station's orbit also took them close enough to the co-ordinates of the European facility, site Echo, but the pictures she took from there told a different story. Her first glimpse of it, years after the impact, showed a small crater. Her only conclusion was to assume that the seismic activity of the impact and the ensuing volcanic eruptions had caused their power supply to lose containment and detonate. As small as it was, their compact nuclear reactor still held a destructive power equal to even a medium-sized warhead from the previous incarnation of the human race. That explosion would have atomized the facility's contents, Annie knew, as she brought up a schematic of the site and ran a simulation of the power source losing containment in a micro-second.

Her assumptions and calculations were wrong.

Knowing that there would never be any contact from that site only made the silence of the African-based survivors even more suspicious, or *anomalous,* in her best sense of the situation. She tried to make contact with their systems, sending out the communication attempt on every pass for an entire day, but each attempt failed.

She fired a single probe, designed for use when they were assessing the conditions on the planet, and guided it to impact near to the biggest settlement; a kind of blunt-force knock on their door to remind them of the presence of other survivors in space.

They weren't responding, or they weren't capable of responding. To save energy, Annie attempted contact once every five thousand, four hundred, and seventy times that the station passed by the almost invisible speck on the surface of the planet. She maintained her constantly evolving algorithms and began to worry about the effects that the ever-increasing risk of the minute friction damage caused by their time in space. Running over her calculations twice and not liking the projected results, she made the choice that it was time to return her precious cargo to Earth.

Deciding that her current operating procedures were not offering the highest survivability rates to her wards sleeping in their tubes, she rewrote her subroutines and began the process to wake up the subjects of the ARC. Annie assessed the topographical charts logged by their onboard telescope to find a suitable landing site near the other survivors.

And after that, she decided, it was time for some company at long last.

~

It was like the worst hangover I'd ever experienced, combined with a sensation that was like a twenty-four-hour food poisoning in fast forward. So many conflicting things went through my head at once that I didn't have a goddamned clue what was happening.

I wanted to throw up, but my head hurt so much I daren't allow my stomach to retch. I felt like I was going to shit my pants, which made me want to throw up even more as I imagined what diarrhea would be like in zero-G. The thought that I was still weightless forced its way through, which made the idea of losing my lunch even worse than shitting my pants. A screeching sound burned my brain like white noise and I opened my mouth to let out a cry of pain. Nothing came out and I started to cough so hard that I began bouncing around with the movements inside the small confines of my cryotube, making me feel so suddenly claustrophobic like I'd been in there for a thousand years. Fighting my way out I flailed around until my brain remembered how to move without that familiar thing called gravity which had been a constant in my life until recently.

Well, I thought, *recently for* me *anyway.*

"Annie," I said, hearing little more than a hoarse, strangled sound escape my mouth but sensing the immediate tone of acknowledgment. I tried again, and still nothing happened.

Then the strangest thing happened. A small cleaning bot, all shiny metal made dull by time in service, floated toward me slowly with a sports bottle of water clasped in a … a hand, like a three-fingered grabbing tool. I don't know why, but it freaked me the hell out.

It stopped in front of me, the smallest hiss of air sounding as it used its built-in compressed air thrusters to maneuver inside the ARC, and I took the bottle and drank.

"Thanks," I croaked, as it about-turned and floated away, mentally kicking myself for talking to something with all the personality and consciousness of a toaster.

I paused then, trying to figure out amidst my pain and confusion, exactly what the hell the robot was doing inside, especially what it was doing bussing tables in my booth. Just as I opened my mouth to ask the one person—thing—that could tell me, the speakers beeped again.

"Good morning, David," Annie said, "your symptoms will subside in a few minutes, but I recommend that you do not try to operate any of the station systems until you are fully recovered."

"Recovered?" I asked, still feeling like my mouth was numb. "Annie, I need to eat something before I throw up," I said, not comprehending how counter-intuitive that sounded. The speaker beeped again, and the robot-waitress returned bearing a sealed foil packet of food, like a space MRE. It hovered there for a second, like it was waiting for a tip, then retreated. I tore the top open to find a cube of preserved cake, still moist which made me surprised somehow, and I chewed it down with difficulty before retrieving the floating water bottle to take another long pull from it.

"You will need to use the bathroom facilities very soon," Annie warned me, like a formally polite, computerized version of someone's mother, "recommend you do not eat or drink any more at this time."

I paused with the bottle halfway to my mouth, one hand keeping me from spinning and one foot wedged to stop the yawing motions. A single blob of water carried on out of the cap and crept toward me, its impetus caused by the sudden stopping of the bottle's motion. I let the single drop hit me softly on the cheek, just as a little more sense penetrated the confused agony I was experiencing.

"Annie," I croaked again, unsure what it was, but certain that something was very, very wrong, "what happened?"

"It's better that I wake up the others first, then I will explain everything," she said, effectively disobeying my instructions.

That's what's wrong, I thought suddenly, *her programming is off.*

"Annie, override," I said, "run diagnostic on la—"

"Dr. Anderson," Annie interrupted with a tone that made me conjure the word *brusque,* "with all due respect, you do not have all the facts. Please wait until I have woken the others up."

"With all due respect?" I asked out loud to myself without saying her name first to activate a voice interface. "Who the hell programmed *that* response?"

"I did," Annie answered, silencing anything else I could think to say, "it is a formal prepositional phrase commonly used by all English-speaking nations. I intended it to be an idiomatic way of disagreeing with you without invoking feelings of confrontation or hostility. Other options available to me were 'with respect' or 'with the greatest respect,' but I decided that the response I used was most appropriate. Now, please comply so that I can continue the resuscitation of the others without using a portion of active memory on this discussion."

With that, a single down-tone came from the speaker which seemed to signify that the conversation was over. I carefully shut my mouth, in case anything else came out which got me in trouble. Sure enough, just as my digestive system woke up as though on a time delay with the rest of me, I turned to pull myself toward the uncomfortable space station bathrooms mouthing the only words I could manage.

What the fuck?

Earth Orbit
January 2, 2948

Amir looked as bad as I had felt. Farnham and Chapman took the news in their strides, neither one seeming to feel the emotional strain that the news caused me, and Hendricks just listened as Annie listed the simplified facts for us.

"Engineer Evans suffered a medical emergency roughly one year and two months after the event. I was unable to rouse trained personnel in a suitable time, so I used a maintenance robot to place him into stasis. I reestablished the parameters of the mission following this incident and took over automated control of the Ark until such time as I required human assistance."

I wasn't the only one to be staring at the speaker with my mouth open, as if the thing she used to talk out of somehow held her consciousness, and we were all raised to look at someone when they spoke to you. She carried on, after the deliberate pause she left for any questions.

"Echo site was destroyed, presumably by power source containment failure at or around the time of the impact event. Radiological poisoning is highly likely in that region. Charlie site was viable," she said before Amir interrupted her in panic.

"Was?" he asked, almost feverish that it too had failed.

"Yes," Annie responded, "it became viable one hundred and eleven years after the event, and has progressed since th—"

All five of us began to speak at once and drowned out what she said next. The noise subsided and Amir asked a simple question.

"Annie, precisely how long have we been in stasis?"

"Precisely?" she asked in a voice which, if it had belonged to a human female, indicated that one eyebrow would be raised.

"Just in years," I said quickly.

"Almost nine hundred and fourteen," Annie shot back. I saw Amir's lips move imperceptibly as he did the calculation in his head before his eyes screwed shut and he forced his head toward his chest.

He held a hand to his closed eyes, as though crying, before he composed himself.

"I'm sorry," he said formally, "I had many friends there."

Nobody quite knew what to say about that, until Annie surprised me again.

"I'm very sorry for your loss, Amir," she said in a sympathetic tone of voice, "please, take a moment if you need to, and we can continue shorty."

"No, no, it's fine," Amir said as he looked back up wearing a resolved if not unconvincing expression. "So you are saying that the other site woke up over eight hundred years ago? And they didn't contact us? And you didn't contact them?"

"They made no attempts to contact this facility," Annie confirmed, "and my attempts to contact them have been unsuccessful."

"Didn't you think to wake one of us up to make that decision?" Hendricks asked softly. "I mean, why did you wait almost a thousand years before doing something?"

"I …" Annie started, "I am sorry, it is hard for me to keep track of time in your sense of the meaning, and I …" She paused again. "I was busy watching them on each pass and didn't think."

All eyes turned to me then, heavy with questions and accusations.

"Hey, it's not my fault," I said, holding up both hands instinctively then having to grab for hold to stop my body from spinning as a result. "Annie? Weren't you programmed with a safeguard to wake someone if you were left on your own, say for example if an engineer was incapacitated?"

"Yes," she answered, "but I rewrote those protocols in order to keep the human cargo safe."

So many emotions were conveyed as small noises right then, until Amir asked me outright.

"So, your perfect computer interface has malfunctioned and kept us frozen for a thousand years?" he said acidly, letting his mask drop a fraction.

"No," I answered feeling numb, "she didn't malfunction, she *evolved*. She isn't just an interface any more, don't you see?"

They didn't, except Farnham and Chapman who seemed to experience the flickering of the lightbulb at the same time.

"No?" Chapman asked incredulously.

"She couldn't have …" Farnham said in little more than a whisper.

"She did," I told them, "Annie became self-aware while we were sleeping, only there won't be any cyborgs travelling back in time to kill us when we're kids."

Chapter 18

Earth Orbit
January 5, 2948

There were still just the five of us awake, as the station really wasn't designed with too many people in mind for comfort. I sat with the others, all crowded around the biggest display we had, and watched as Annie replayed over four million images in rapid sequence like the world's biggest flip-book.

We watched as hundreds of years of civilization rose and fell, ebbed and flowed outwards from the hole in the ground which we knew led to the massive facility buried there. It was designed to remain buried, only empty as a kind of emergency shelter which provided the power. We each reacted to individual things we saw; brief flashes of things we recognized like an earth-moving vehicle seen on one image before it disappeared in the next instant.

We watched the whole thing through, taking almost six hours to go through the four and a half million images played on the screen so many per second. It was weird, like my eyes would recognize something or focus on a particular movement, and although it was gone in a split-second, it was like I could still see it; like my eyeballs had a limited memory capacity.

"So why aren't they responding to contact?" Amir asked again to nobody in particular, as though voicing his thoughts and worries was a productive method of nurturing ideas.

"I have hypothesized different reasons for that," Annie said, without chiming to indicate that her interface program was activated. That still frightened me a little, as much as the thought of having an actual child did, that my creation was thinking for itself.

"I can only surmise that the ANII"—she used the interface program initials for what was once her equal and now just a machine in her opinion—"has either malfunctioned or has been intentionally programmed to ignore my attempts to make contact. I am unable to take direct control without plugging in on a hard line to that facility. Attempts to access their systems via radio and long-range digital means have been blocked, so a wireless attempt nearby would also likely fail," she said, betraying that she had tried to find a way to fix the communication issue without help.

Well I certainly didn't program that, I told myself.

I fought the urge to interrupt, like me asking how she formulated and programmed her problem-solving algorithms was the most important thing in—or near—the world right now.

"So, it's either knackered," said Hendricks with a heavy sub-text of something to do with a stiff upper lip, "or they are simply ignoring us?"

"Yes," Annie answered simply, leaving a silence in the chamber we occupied.

"Well," Amir said as he pushed himself away from the console to float free of the foot straps in some space-like approximation of slapping his hands on his desk and launching into action, "I want to see more topographical scans and gather surface data before we do anything. Annie?"

"Yes?" she said, making everyone feel slightly uneasy as that word they had been using for so many years always prompted a chime in response and not the tone of voice of an unimpressed spouse.

"Launch the surface and atmospheric drones," he said. When he heard no response he added, "please."

There was a pause, then a slight shudder as a muted double thudding sound reverberated along the entire structure.

"Probes launched," Annie announced, "adjusting position to compensate for launches … Done."

"Annie?" I asked, not waiting for a response tone. "Why did you do that?"

"Do what, David?" she responded.

"Why did you tell us what you were doing with the orbit adjustment after the launch?" I knew she was programmed to do it, because I'd personally spent a month programming the subroutines which allowed her to control the orbit of the station automatically, but I'd never programmed her to explain what she was doing.

"I am undertaking a study of five human males and monitoring their vital signs in response to events which they do not fully understand," she said. "I have already determined that the emotional state and physiological stress responses are significantly lower when verbal confirmations are provided, shall I continue to do this?"

I was dumbstruck. Not only was she *able* to even do that, but she was already studying *us* to be more streamlined. Exchanging looks with the others, who saw her explanation as reasonable and rational, I saw that they really didn't understand why I was so shocked.

"Yes, please do," I said, seeing Hendricks turn to Amir.

"If we are going to the surface," he said seriously, "I need my team out of the freezer and briefed."

~

Hendricks had woken, or got Annie to wake, the other six members of Sierra Team and helped them all in turn as they adjusted to being awake and in permanent free fall. Like the professional he was, he saw to their immediate needs and prioritized each one like a battlefield triage system. He made sure they were all set, and allowed them to gather themselves and come around in their own time. Even the toughest people he had ever met could not simply shrug off almost a thousand years spent frozen, and it was like each year they had spent in stasis cost them a few agonizing seconds of extreme hangover symptoms to repay.

When they were all fully conscious and on the same planet, or above the same planet, Hendricks briefed them as one. He kept it short and sweet, and to their credit, and very telling of their characters not to mention the years of training they had endured, not one of them melted down over the additional almost millennia they were expecting to have passed by below. They were professionals, and they wanted to know what job he had in store for them.

Amir and the others had pored over the imagery provided by Annie, giving us an acceptable landing area only a dozen miles from the largest remaining, sprawling colony on the planet. The original plan had always been to use the pods as an enclave for when they got back down to the planet; they were designed to land within centimeters of one another to form a wall. Two of the pods were specially constructed to act as a kind of gateway, and their contents spread out to become doors which would operate and effectively seal the ring of space-age materials. It was a concept ages old: circling the wagons. The pod containing the power source would land centrally, along with a couple of others, and heavy cabling would snake out to power our ringed fortifications. That pod would also contain Annie's central processing core because, you know, who *doesn't* need a now-sentient super-computer helping them out.

They all filed into their two drop-ship modules, from the outside looking the same as all the others, carrying heavy bags of weaponry and equipment, and settled in for the ride down. Annie would land them in the precise spots next to each other to form a tiny section of the planned defenses, but after that they were on their own until they sent word to begin the reverse of their initial exodus.

They left without fanfare, Hendricks merely offering me a nod of acknowledgement before he floated inside and sealed his tube. The other side of that door was about to become the only thing separating me from outer space, and despite the technical reassurances, I got my precious ass back to where I could watch them go in relative safety. That launch, narrated by Annie for our benefit to prevent our stress levels from rising, apparently, reverberated around the station with less concussion than the launch of the probes which had declared the surface fit for human habitation, like we didn't already realize that us humans had been active there for the last eight hundred years.

Earth

January, 9

Hendricks had endured the drop with Magda and Weber, while Geiger, Nathalie, Stevens, and their other Brit, Jones, followed thirty-one minutes later in the other pod as the station made its next pass. The three other conscious members of the crew aboard the ARC watched through the tiny portholes as the big, white chunks of their modular space station floated away seeming slow but in truth hurtling at incredible speeds.

The reentry into the atmosphere was as bumpy as the rocket burn of their upward journey, but none of Sierra Team had experienced that as they were in a state of frozen slumber. Nobody said a word, but the grunts and tight-lipped release of air from their lungs gave as much situational stress away as they were willing to show. The release of the three canopies was the next big jolt, and Annie gave them fair warning along with a countdown to expect it. It felt to Hendricks like what he would expect a helicopter crash, a mild one at least, would feel like. Their specially designed seats cushioned the inertia by compressing on heavy springs to prevent them from stepping off onto solid ground a good deal shorter than when they started. The microbursts of compressed air helped Annie steer them down, and all they had to do was hold on until they hit the dirt in the flat area chosen as their settlement.

Struggling out of their harnesses and then their bulky space suits, they pulled on their tactical gear and climbed out of the top hatch for their first look at their home planet in its new form.

The first thing that hit Hendricks was the humidity. It wasn't so much the heat as the heavy quality to the air which took his breath away and instantly made a film of sweat appear on his skin. Raising his new, next-generation HK assault rifle, he scanned a full circle from his kneeling position atop the pod before calling, "Clear." He settled himself to make the drop to the ground, followed by Magda, his former counter-terrorism surveillance expert, and the big German, Weber.

The environment was tropical and made him remember the swamps of the southern states or the jungles of South America where he spent time in both leisure and employment.

"Jesus," cursed Weber, "it is hotter than the hells here." Magda smiled at the big German's discomfort but seemed not to show that the weather affected her. She had spent her career staying still and silent, invisible even, in worse conditions than she now experienced. Hendricks took a knee and removed his tactical gear to strip down to a tan T-shirt before replacing the heavy equipment, then took up his weapon again as the others followed suit.

"Annie," he said onto his radio, "ETA for the others?"

Annie responded after a second with, "Second pod inbound, ETA sixteen minutes and eighteen seconds."

Hendricks thought, calculating that they wanted to be clear of their pod by a hundred meters at least before the rest of his team landed. Turning slightly and nodding to Magda before switching back to his field of fire, he saw his peripheral vision blur with her movement. She slung her weapon behind her, the same as they all carried, and dug into a hard case to unfold the wings of a drone. It powered up instantly and shot skyward on a pre-programmed path to settle at a hundred feet above them, before the tablet that she powered up gave her real-time information.

"Tree line," she said after staring hard at the screen for a few beats, "raised outcrop one hundred fifteen meters north by northwest," before gaining it visually and pointing the way. Hendricks nodded to her, then to Weber who rose to his feet and set off, weapon scanning left and right as he went. Hendricks allowed Magda to fall in behind him, weapon still slung and eyes darting between their environment and the readout, then fell in as what he called their tail-end Charlie.

Reaching the raised hump covered in what looked a lot like palm trees, they settled into an all-round defense and waited the remaining six minutes plus for the arrival of the others. A curious whistling sound reached them first, as the heavy foliage prevented much upward vision, and that whistling registered as a heavy object hissing toward the earth under the guidance of three canopies and the bursts of compressed air fired out of the thruster ports to steer it. They watched in awe as the pod slowed and settled directly adjacent to their own, for the three 'chutes hanging limp to retract into their compartments, then waited another minute for the top hatch of that second pod to pop.

"Pod two, Hendricks," the staunch Brit said confidently into the radio.

"Two, Stevens, we're in one piece. You all good?" came the reply.

"All good," Hendricks responded, not bothering to keep the relief out of his words. That was one of the reasons they gelled so well, as every other member of the team felt as though they were under the command of their favorite uncle. "Shirtsleeves only," Hendricks explained before adopting a mocking German accent. "Veber says it is hotter zan ze hells here," he finished with an appalling impression of their biggest team mate.

They watched from their outcrop as the remaining four members of Sierra climbed out and dropped to the ground, then jogged back over to them. Hands were clasped, nods were exchanged, and Annie hailed the entire net to address them.

"Readings from your drone indicate no movement or life signs in this area. Are you in agreement that I begin to launch the remaining pods to this location?" she asked. Hendricks looked around his team, non-verbally checking for any concerns or objections to be raised and meeting nods from everyone.

"Yes, Annie," he said, "please bring everyone else down."

Chapter 19

BUMP IN THE NIGHT

The pods came steadily, each one being released every half hour as the station passed them in orbit high above, and landed consistently throughout the daylight hours so as to allow the ground team to get at least some sleep.

Stevens and Geiger complained loudly that they had slept long enough, but Hendricks wouldn't allow an overly ambitious haste to jeopardize the operation. Annie kept the ground team in regular contact with the others still aboard and landed the pods expertly.

Within twenty-four hours of the first space-based survivors touching down, the ring of pods was close to completion. They planned to set up their basic shelters inside the ring when it was formed and seal it tight before beginning to defrost any of the survivors, but the laborious process of unpacking the supply crates from the pods not holding human cargo was not something that seven people alone could do.

To ease the excitement of his team, Hendricks ordered the small patch on higher ground be cleared and set up as an OP—observation post, or guard tower overlooking the approach to their rapidly-forming enclave. Weber, Stevens, Geiger, and Jones all volunteered for the task, the two Americans eager to employ their bushcraft skills and the German and the Brit just wanting to be out in the field doing something useful. All of them had an overwhelming sense of having been cooped up for too long, as though their frozen bodies somehow held a feeling of having been in a car for an extended journey. Hendricks stayed with the two female members of his team; all three of them suited more to methodical, logical planning over instant action.

By the end of their second day back on Earth, the ring was complete and only three units remained in space. Of those three, one would bring down the last of the human cargo but as Annie would already have had to leave, it would need to be piloted. Farnham took that job, and of course his pod was the only one of them to land out of place.

If they could see it from space again, they would see a near perfect ring of scorched white metal cylinders, with a cloverleaf in the middle where one leaf was ever so slightly awry.

Annie showed another side to her new personality, and just as the others did, she gave him shit for it.

The eleven of them met in the center of the wide circle and quietly congratulated each other. The circumstances of their survival were vastly different to what any of them had expected, but that did not dull the sense of achievement that they felt collectively, and there was a buzz of unspoken excitement as though they were pioneers of their race. They were, and they faced as much uncertainty as any traveler to an unknown place anywhere in history, but they were well-equipped and there were no useless mouths to feed amongst them.

"Annie," Amir said, still looking up as though he were addressing a speaker fixed to a wall. Hearing her deliberate chime of response via the radio he wore on a tactical vest that looked just as natural on him as a Saville Row made suit did he say, "shall we begin the second phase? Engineering staff first, if you please?"

Annie said nothing, but their radios chimed in acknowledgement. She began to wake the prioritized list of personnel, talking to each of them as she roused them gently and allowed them to regain consciousness more slowly than the first of them in a measured test to ease their transitions into consciousness. One by one, the pod hatches popped open and wary eyes blinked at the sunlight.

I'd asked Annie which pod Elliot was in, as he would be one of the first to wake and oversee the majority of the people being brought out of cryo. She told me which pod, which actually meant nothing to me.

"Where is that?" I asked, getting used to the fact that she was always listening via the radio without me having to key the mic or say her name and wait for a response. In reply, she simply flashed the lights on the outside of a pod about thirty paces from me. I thanked her and walked over to climb inside and pass Elliot a bottle of water as he reeled and coughed in a state of confusion like he was blind drunk.

"Easy, buddy," I told him as his eyes slowly focused on me.

"How long?" he asked groggily with a croaking voice before taking a pained swig from the bottle.

"Not sure you wanna know, man," I said carefully, wearing an expression that I hoped would tell him half the story. His eyes stayed

153

fixed on me, waiting for an answer which I was forced to give with a sigh.

"A little over nine hundred," I said simply. He choked on the water and began another coughing fit which lasted longer than was comfortable to watch. Eventually he lapsed back into silence and drank a little more before rubbing his face hard.

"We were never supposed to be under for that long," he said in a small voice, "did everyone make it?"

"Yes," I told him, "even one of the engineers who was taken seriously ill when we were up there. Annie put him in a freezer by herself and took over control of the station …" I said, trailing off and waiting for the seriousness of what I had told him to sink in.

"She …" he said slowly as he stared off into nothing, "she what?"

"Yeah," I told him, "I wouldn't have believed it myself if I didn't know it was true, but my little girl's all grown up now," I said, hoping to ease him into the knowledge that as he slept, his creations were monitored and controlled by a sentient artificial intelligence who had discovered self-awareness without us.

Elliot tried to form words but managed only a series of noises as he couldn't decide what to say. Waking up after almost a thousand years to find out that a computer had learned to make its own decisions was way worse than finding yourself with a killer hangover in someone else's bed and no idea how you got there.

"Come on, buddy," I said as I stood and offered him a hand, "come see Earth up close again."

Twenty-three miles away to their north, separated by thick jungle and one river, a boy ran through a crowd dodging around and sometimes under obstructions before he neared the front and climbed the side of a shack to see and hear what was happening.

A man stood on a raised platform, the same one they used for public punishments, where his brother had once been whipped for stealing, and called out to the assembly.

"Yes," he shouted, "the legends appear to be true. There were others up there"—he paused to look up and point at nothing high up in the sky—"and we all saw them coming down here. The day after tomorrow, at dawn, I will lead a war party south to find them. For now, the light is fading … Close the gates!" he yelled, and the boy watched the flurry of activity as everyone melted away to lock down for the coming darkness, as they had done for generations. The livestock were herded inside the high town walls, guards stood alert in their towers beside the big lamps mounted at regular intervals bathing the ground beneath the walls with a purple hue, and everyone prayed that the things would not come.

"Is that the medical shelter?" Chapman shouted over to the others who were seeming to struggle with what part of the pop-up shelter was the front. Weber looked at the red cross printed on the section of material in his hands and shouted back that he was pretty sure it was. The sun was beginning to set and all of them were back inside the enclave with the gates closed. Stevens and Geiger were sat on the gate pods, each cradling a rifle and keeping a watchful eye on the ground ahead. They had all been to places near the equator, so both knew how quickly the transition between night and day happened.

Shelters had been erected which would at least give them somewhere to sleep and eat in relative comfort, and they all reckoned that a sleeping bag on an inflated mat was way better than climbing back into their cramped flight seats in the pods. They had unpacked the supplies, with Annie's help, from where they all were stowed away and vacuum-sealed. One of the guys thawed out that day was like a dazed zombie, as he swirled a wooden spoon in a pot resting on a camp stove. They had emptied out a dozen packets of the space MREs and planned to dig in together for a meal before they slept. In addition to the eleven of them who had been conscious when they got to the planet, they had woken another ten from cryo to help get the camp set up before everyone else was brought out. Of those others, there were more than a few who weren't mission-critical, as almost everyone important had brought passengers along as their fee and the place needed tidying up before they were brought out.

Walkways were created by laying waffle-board panels, and the parachute canopies were designed to be linked eventually to create a roof over framework that was packed tightly in one of the pods. The pods themselves were designed to have their inward facing walls cut away to create more permanent structures to allow the separation of family units, but for now they were busy creating a pioneer camp safely inside their walls.

"Annie?" Hendricks said softly, knowing that his radio would pick up the words and connect the computer to him. His earpiece alone sounded a chime, streamlining the communication process to let him know she was listening. "Can you take over control of the patrol drones to keep watch for us?"

"Yes," she said instantly before a short pause, "drones launching. I have contacted your sentries to inform them to return."

"Thanks," Hendricks replied, marveling at how she had anticipated his request meant that he could get his two men back inside and eating hot food for the first time in about a thousand years, "but next time, could you run that kind of thing past me first?"

"Of course," Annie said, "I apologize for being presumptuous, I was merely trying to streamline the process I anticipated."

"I know, and you were right," Hendricks said in an equally apologetic tone, "it's just that I might have other plans that you aren't aware of sometimes. Not a criticism, I'm just trying to streamline too."

Just inside of a minute later, the two American soldiers jogged back over and ducked into the large semi-rigid shelter they were all occupying and sat down to enjoy a meal with the entire group.

Anderson noticed a peculiarity among them at that moment. He and the other civilians of their Ark were all in relaxation mode, with one guy even wearing a pair of ridiculous sandals which looked like an oversized rubber strainer, but the Sierra people were all still wearing their boots, and all of them had their weapons no further than a short grab away. Sure, they gave some concessions to comfort, like unfastening their tactical vests and putting their feet up, but all of them stayed ready to rock at any second.

After a meal and some discussion, the welcome suggestion for everyone to turn in came from Amir and they climbed into their sleeping bags. The heat abated greatly during the night, they had found, but they were sure that the humidity would rise again as soon as the dawn broke.

"Caution, movement alert outside of perimeter," came the rushed, computerized tones of Annie. She sounded like she was in a panic, which didn't fill Anderson with any kind of confidence. Panic breeds panic, he remembered Stevens telling him when they were creeping around the ass-end of nowhere on a Kentucky mountainside so long ago. She had spoken through the radios at high volume, serving only to alarm everyone in the tent as they woke to the rushed movements of the team members who were already throwing on their equipment, betraying that they were ready, even when they were asleep.

"Annie, report please," Hendricks said in clipped but polite tones as he breathed in to secure the Velcro flaps of his heavy vest.

"Large body of movement, western edge near the gate ..." She trailed off. If she were human, a person would be forgiven for thinking that she was nervous or unsure of what she was saying, but to those who understood how her programming worked, they realized she was calculating and hypothesizing as to what the readings she got from the drones actually meant.

"Large single contact?" Nathalie asked in her richly French-accented English, a hint of steel in her tone.

"Unknown," Annie responded. "Calculating."

Hendricks glanced up to see that his team was ready, then turned to Amir who had donned his vest more slowly but stood ready nonetheless. A silent communication flashed between the two men as their eyes met, and Amir nodded before turning back to the others and raising his voice.

"Okay, I need everyone else ready and on me in the center, let's go people!"

With a last glance back at his team, Hendricks charged his assault rifle and hit the door release button to lead his team into the darkness beyond. The heavy quality of the air took their breath away immediately. Although far less severe than in the daytime, with the lower temperature of the night it just seemed to be more stifling, more suffocating than it did in daylight.

The next thing to crash into their consciousness was the sound. It was a sound that was both natural and at the same time wholly wrong; like a supernatural screeching, like nails down a chalkboard. A high-pitched, almost metallic hum which made the air vibrate.

"What the hell is that?" Stevens called out. "Cicadas?"

"I ain't never heard a swarm that size," Geiger responded to him in a lower tone as he moved forward crouched over his weapon sight as the barrel swung through the full range of his fire sector.

"Annie," Hendricks said coolly, "can you identify the noise?"

"Negative," Annie responded instantly, her tone changing to match the hard professionalism of the team. "Stevens could be right; the sound profile matches the file I have of cicadas by sixty-eight percent."

Sixty-eight percent, Hendricks thought, *that's a hell of a margin for error if whatever is making that bloody noise isn't cicadas.*

Racking his brains for everything he knew about the bugs as he stalked forward sweeping his own sector at the lead, he summarized that he didn't know much. Swarms? That didn't sound good, but he was certain they weren't harmful to humans at least.

"Annie?" he said as he called a silent halt near the gateway with a raised fist. "Does the sound profile match anything which could be harmful to us? Or …" He paused, thinking of another way to say what was on his mind and failing. "Or *carnivorous*?"

"Calculating," Annie said in their earpieces, no doubt part of her self-written stress-reduction protocols by keeping the people informed of the steps.

"Other known forms of insect are known for creating a similar sound, however nothing on file matches the criteria for risk, other than some form of poisonous beetles or ants," she reported.

"Great," Nathalie grumbled, louder than she intended. For a woman who had faced off with dozens of armed terrorists and held under such pressure as scoring headshots on suicide bombers before they could flip a switch, she still felt her spine crawl uncomfortably at the thought of bugs.

"Executive decision," Hendricks snapped professionally, "nobody goes outside until we know what it or they are. Annie, can you get closer with the drone to record footage?"

"Negative, lighting is insufficient and night-vision cannot discern a single body of the mass," she answered, making Hendricks imagine a cool controller watching drone feed imagery and reporting to the ground team via radio. Only she wasn't doing that, because she wasn't even a she and there was no control room.

Hendricks thought for a moment. "Annie, how close are they to the top of the walls?"

"They are less than halfway, and do not seem capable of scaling the surface."

Hendricks looked up at the top of the wall and dropped his rifle on its sling before his earpiece hummed once more.

"Hendricks," Annie said in an authoritative tone, "recommend you *do not* scale the wall for a closer look."

He opened his mouth to respond, to ask if she could read his thoughts, before another sound penetrated the din which surrounded their compound; another drone had been launched and was hovering near them with the camera focused on the team.

Hendricks closed his mouth and picked up his weapon again before turning to his team and taking a knee. They crowded in and followed suit.

"Recommendations?" he asked.

Before anyone could answer, Annie spoke to all of them via their earpieces. "Recommend you do nothing; stay down, stay quiet and do not provoke the swarm."

"Then what?" Weber asked. "We hide every night without knowing what the hell they are?"

"Negative," Annie said, her voice bordering dangerously on the sensation of being 'disappointed.' "Consolidate and reinforce during daylight and set a trap for a test subject. Information suggests that the swarm is nocturnally active only."

"I can do that," Stevens said, looking at Geiger and Weber who both nodded in agreement.

"Okay," Hendricks said, taking charge again and realizing that the computer had effectively decided for them, "Magda and Dieter take the north point and patrol ten o'clock to two o'clock, Stevens and Kurt take the south east, two o'clock to six, Nathalie and Jones, six to ten, understood?" he asked as he looked at each pair in turn to receive confirmation of his simple orders to divide their enclosed circle into three patrol zones. It seemed that Annie understood also.

"I have activated the inward-facing LEDs on top of the relevant pods to indicate fields of responsibility," she announced helpfully, "they are not visible from outside of the compound."

Hendricks had to admit that was actually really a good idea, as one of the hardest things he had ever found with teaching inexperienced personnel with firearms was what he called the LOE: their limit of exploitation. Referred to by many other terms—your sector, your arc of fire, your area of responsibility—it simply meant the place where your gun was supposed to be active so as to not interfere with others. In this case, dividing a one-hundred-and-twenty-degree arc inside of an unlit circle over what was about two acres of flat ground wasn't something so easy to do, and the three parts of his team could easily find themselves straying into each other's territory. Annie's simple recognition and resolving of that problem happened in a flash and was useful.

Bloody useful, Hendricks thought as his mind wandered slightly with the tactical advantages that Annie could provide in different circumstances. Shaking that away he deployed his troops.

"Go now," he said, "I'll bring you NVGs."

As he walked back to the central tent to give the others a brief summary and hope that they didn't panic, Annie's voice sounded in his ear.

"Hendricks, this is a private channel between us," she said softly, almost conspiratorially, "I have deployed a drone over each pair and the swarm seems to have circled our compound twice. They appear to be moving off now; direction due north by northeast."

"Thank you," Hendricks said, appearing to anyone watching as though he were having a one-sided conversation with himself. "Fancy speculating?" he asked her quietly as he was still thirty paces from the tent. He heard the chime in his ear that told him she was computing something. It was like her artificial intelligence way of streamlining the words, "Wait one."

"Speculation has a high percentage of being partially or significantly inaccurate," she said, as though reading her own disclaimer, "but best hypothesis at this time is that there were species of insects on Earth which survived the event and have mutated to exhibit different appearances and behaviors."

"Great, mutant bugs?" Hendricks hissed in exasperation.

"Yes," Annie said patiently, "however we do not know if they represent a risk to us, or what level of risk."

Hendricks entered the tent, holding up both hands and trying his hardest to seem casual and unconcerned. He put on his, *it's just standard procedure, folks,* face and smiled at them.

"Relax, everyone," he started, knowing that the truth in its currently incomplete state would cause panic, "turns out there are some animals moving about outside but they just circled us and moved off. As a precaution only, I'll keep Sierra Team on the ground until daybreak. Please, everyone stay inside, Mr. Weatherby can contact me on the radio should the situation in here change, okay?" He made reassuring eye contact with everyone he could, then nodded to Amir for the man to join him for a private conversation.

In brief, single lines, he filled him in on the facts as he had them and recited their current and immediate future plans.

"We continue as we were by day, but nobody goes outside the compound unless I directly authorize it." His eyes asked for confirmation that Amir understood and wouldn't try to pull any *I'm in charge here* bullshit. Amir understood, agreed, and acknowledged the orders.

Hendricks gave him a gentle slap on the shoulder before rummaging in a hard case to bring out seven pairs of compact night vision goggles and went back out into the dark.

Chapter 20

REALITY CHECK

As if finding out that the world was going to end by way of an aster-oid strike, and spending a good few years working solidly to make sure I and as many others as possible could survive it, and then wak-ing up expecting a hundred years to have passed and finding out it's close to thousand wasn't enough, I now had this shit to deal with.

I was literally just about getting my head around the fact that we were pioneers back on Earth and starting from scratch, that one of our sites went boom over nine hundred years ago, and that the others were seemingly fine but not talking to us, when I find out that there are big swarms of goddamned bugs running around at night.

I like to think that I'm fairly normal in that sense; the dislike of all things creepy and crawly is a perfectly natural state for mankind because, well, because the little bastards are creepy. And crawly. Every time I think about it, my skin crawls all over and I end up doing that weird dance thing everyone does. Hendricks calls it 'someone walking over his grave' and doesn't seem to think that's at all disturbing.

I don't know why I was asked to join in, but Hendricks and Chapman along with Geiger and Stevens all huddled up around a small tablet in one of the shelters.

"Gentlemen," Hendricks began with his usual British jauntiness, "the problem is simple: we wish to construct a kind box trap to secure a live subject from the swarm of bugs that passed us by last night. Thoughts?"

I'll be honest, my first thought was, *Urgh, hell no,* then I got a hold of myself and tried to focus on the task. The two survivalist experts, or crazy-woodland-prepper-nut-jobs if I was being silently unkind, were bouncing off one another as they came up with a plan. As they talked, Hendricks and Chapman watching intently, I opened my mouth to offer an easier solution. Just as I did, and before I could even breathe in to voice my interruption, our radios all spoke at once.

"Gentlemen, if I may offer a solution?" Annie asked politely but confidently.

"You want us to put a small cryopod outside and let you activate it?" I said quickly, if only to prove to myself that my brain was still a useful tool that hadn't been replaced by my own creation.

"Yes, David," she said smoothly, "any pod will suffice, I just need a sensory input and power supply."

"Wont freezing it prevent us from being able to study it?" Chapman asked, his eyes already going out of focus as he was distracted by the problem of building a sensor unit.

"No," Annie responded, the tone of her voice sounding slightly off as though I hadn't heard that specific intonation before.

Could she be rewriting her communication subroutines now? Or is her personality evolving?

"I can use a reduced amount of anesthetic to pacify the unknown organism, which should allow for experimentation and study," she finished.

"I can rig a movement sensor in the foot end of a tube, which should show you when something is properly inside for you to trap it. Will that work?" Chapman asked.

"If you wire it into the sensor protocols of the tube, or attach a wireless device, I can work with that," Annie told him.

Nods showed slowly around our little group, until Stevens asked the question it seemed we were all thinking of.

"Bait?" he asked, glancing up to see reactions.

"Given the behavior of the mass," Annie said after having let the silence run its course, "I believe that bait would not be necessary."

Somehow, I was a little thankful for that, as bait implied that we were trying to trap a predator, and I didn't want to think that there were swarms of predators out past our walls in the inky darkness.

Nightfall came, and a pod was laid out just away from the wall near to the gate, with a power cable running from the nearest of the landed sections of our old space station. Chapman had fitted a tracker unit, the same as we all wore on out wrists, to a motion sensor device which was part of the array that could be made into our future perimeter defenses. Annie tested it, simulating the time it would take to secure the pod after she received a signal, and settled on closing the heavy, see-through panel halfway to cut down on the time needed. It was set, and we all retreated inside to wait.

Annie had all but two of the drones up in the air, cycling them in and out in a staggered routine so that none of them ever went below thirty percent power. The two units on charge could be deployed to cover the ground team should they need it, and everyone shut up tight for the darkness.

The others hadn't been idling all day, as the medic tent was now fully operational, and another fifteen people came out of their freezers. One of them was a stunning medical doctor, all glamorous smiles and hair that seemed to swish as though it was a catwalk model in its own right. She was a lot older than she looked, and trust me she looked great, but she carried it with a kind of playful grace which spoke simultaneously of a young spirit and the benefit of experience. I heard her talking with the others, re-jigging some kind of priority system and getting other specialists fully acclimated from frozen to hot and humid before they dealt with their emergency. It took me a second to figure out what emergency it could be, panicking for a second that someone had gotten hurt or worse, attacked by a swarm of flesh-eating cicadas, until it dawned on me that they were talking about the engineer guy who Annie had thrown into cryo to prevent him dying on board the ARC.

Pushing thoughts about sick people and me needing a full physical out of my head, I ate with the others from a wide selection of re-heated, flash-frozen goodness, and took a shower in one of the temporary set ups which drew water from the atmosphere and both heated and purified it during the day using sunlight alone.

After that, I joined Chapman, Amir, and Hendricks as we watched the screens which folded out of a large suitcase as a kind of mobile control center. I mentioned as much and ended up feeling like a dumbass because that's exactly what the thing was. I'd been feeling pretty damn edgy since the swarm circled us the previous night, so I'd kept a closer eye on where the members of Sierra Team were, just in case I needed to hide behind them at any point. I found a couple dozing, no doubt recharging their batteries in case they had to spring into action in the night, saw two on the wall watching the setting sun, and even found the massive German guy, Weber, sketching on a notepad with a pencil. Dressed now in clean clothes and having re-laced my boots, I struggled to get comfortable with the sidearm strapped to my right hip. I was unaccustomed to its weight and bulk and kept knocking it on things. Leaning over so that I didn't get the butt digging into my skin, I watched the screens.

"Why don't we rig some lights?" Chapman offered.

"You really want to announce our presence here just yet?" Amir countered.

"UV lights?" I offered.

"Possibly," Hendricks said, his tone of voice implying that only a portion of his consciousness was on the conversation, "it certainly would help with the clarity of our night optics and that of the drones."

"I'll get to it, then," Chapman said, his own mind wandering no doubt to who and what he needed to make it work.

"Annie, what about the automated defense grid?" Amir asked out loud.

"Automated defense grid can be activated, however ammunition is at a premium," she said. "I would advise against any direct defensive action until we have studied th—"

"Yes, we are all in agreement on that front," Hendricks interjected, "I believe Mr. Weatherby would like to know how long it would take to set up."

"Eight hours, utilizing a team of five engineering personnel," she shot back as soon as he had finished speaking.

"Okay," Hendricks said, "we can get that done before nightfall, but I want it powered down unless I give authority, understood?"

Our circle nodded their agreement, and a single up-tone sounded through Hendricks' radio.

~

Just beyond the tree line overlooking their metal-ringed camp, ten young men and women watched in silence. They saw nothing, no movement outside of the scorched white pods, marked by their re-entry into Earth's atmosphere. Occasional noises washed up to their vantage point, and just after the sun reached its peak in the sky they saw the distant movement of people atop the walls, building small tripods on which they mounted box shapes with protruding barrels.

"Harrison," one of them hissed to the immobile leader of the party as he stared resolutely, unblinkingly at the camp, "we need to move soon to be home before nightfall."

Harrison, tall and scarred, thought about what she had said. He gave no indication that he had heard, less still that he was thinking about it or heeding her words. The air of arrogant mystery kept him above them and in charge, he believed.

"We move," he said finally, "and we come back tomorrow."

~

As darkness fell, and the last of the twenty-six automated guns were secured on top of pods at set distances apart for their firing arcs to interlock, everyone retreated inside the main tent which was becoming more of a camp mess hall than the sleeping compartment it was the previous night. As I washed my hands at the designated hygiene station and joined the line for some chow, a familiar figure fell in beside me.

"Cat!" I exclaimed, meeting my lunchtime watcher again for the first time in a year. Or at least what felt like a year for me.

"Dr. Anderson," she said coyly with a smile that seemed as warm and welcoming as a tropical beach, "how are you?"

"Me?" I said, flustered. "I'm fine. What about you? When did you get out of the freezer?"

"This morning," she said, "not an experience I want to repeat, let me tell you."

I looked at her, drinking in that levelling goodness she brought me every day when I was trapped in my lab in Texas arguing with a computer system. She looked different, somehow, like I was just seeing her for the first time or maybe she was letting her true self shine through. God, she was cute, not that I hadn't noticed her before but now was just a whole new level.

Maybe a thousand years on ice made me horny or something, but I just couldn't get over the change I saw in her. Remembering that she'd spoken to me, I recovered in time.

"Oh, yeah," I blurted out, "I didn't know if I was going to throw up or shi—" I managed to stop myself in time and made a series of embarrassing noises as I tried to style it out, "or, just, uh, pass out or something …"

Cat smiled at my awkwardness, enjoying watching me make an ass of myself. It was then that I noticed what seemed different about her. Of all the times I had seen her, she was always wearing casual clothing like jeans and a light sweater or tank top. Now, with it finally dawning on me like the dumbass I was, I saw that she was wearing scrubs. Not the white scrubs that we all had for going into cryo, but the surgical type. Blue and industrial, wearing trail shoes under them, I realized what she was.

"You're a doctor?" I asked, just when she probably began to feel awkward with me staring down at her chest. She laughed, patting my arm gently.

"I'm a nurse," she said, "didn't you know that?"

"No," I said honestly, "I didn't."

"Well," she went on as the line shuffled forward slightly, "I'm trained in a bit of everything now after all that time at the facility, but I'm a psychiatric nurse as well as being qualified in surgical procedures."

A psychiatric nurse … well, now things made a little more sense as to why she stopped by to make sure I ate every day. She was making sure I wasn't going insane. Nice. Pretending I had absorbed that fact and not connected any dots that made me look like a fruitcake, I changed the subject.

"So, what do you think?" I asked, seeing her look of confusion before adding, "Of Earth? Pretty warm, huh?"

She smiled again and agreed that it was pretty hot.

"Hotter than home, anyways," she said, making me consider a question I'd been so self-absorbed I'd never thought to ask.

"Where is home for you?" I asked.

"Cameron Parish, Louisiana, originally. Down in the bayou," she answered, cranking up the dial on her accent that had been diluted by living in so many other places for her training. "You ever been?"

I didn't know how to tell her that Texas was the furthest I'd ever been from my native north east, and that my knowledge of the Louisiana culture was pretty poor. Deciding that the best course of action was not to try and demonstrate that lack of knowledge, I tried a new approach.

"Never. Tell me about home?"

Cat sighed, almost wistful at the memories my question caused to flood back to her before answering.

"I miss real Creole food," she said, her accent plucking at my brain and triggering something inside me, as though I'd been too wrapped up in programming to really see or hear her when I was buried in subroutines. "I miss the street parties from growing up, and real Haitian food. I guess that'll never happen again."

She seemed saddened by her reverie, and I instantly felt bad for prompting it.

"Don't get upset," I tried, failing to invoke another sweet smile from her, "you're keeping that part alive, aren't you? I mean, just by being here, just by surviving it all?"

Another sad smile washed across her face, giving me the obvious impression that I hadn't made a good impression on her. Just as the silence tipped over the edge into the uncomfortable bracket, another voice called out over the gentle din in the shelter.

"Catarina!" I looked up to locate the source of the voice, finding myself looking directly at the tall, blonde doctor who seemed to embody class. Cat looked away, responding with, "Dr. Warren," and raising a small hand.

The doctor came toward her and placed a hand on her forearm. "Call me Kelly, I've told you," she said in friendly admonishment. Cat smiled to accept the reproof before remembering my company.

"Kelly," she said more formally as her accent faded once more, "this is Dr. David Anderson, he's the guy who created Annie," she said as she looked to me. "David, Kelly Warren, MD."

I shook the tall woman's hand politely, not gripping it like I would a man's but finding her squeezing back.

"Pleasure," she said, "Dr. Anderson, you don't mind if I borrow Catarina, do you? I need to discuss an important task we have in the morning."

"By all means," I said with a smile, hiding the crush of attractive company being taken away from me. The two women spoke fast in low voices and I could only glean the basics of what they discussed as I turned away to catch up with the gap in the line ahead which had formed as I was embarrassing myself.

Casting an eye back to try and catch a glimpse of the two women, I saw Amir sitting in a quiet corner with Hayley Cole. As I watched, she smiled shyly and brushed her hair behind her right ear with her fingertips.

Well, I thought, *at least that's out in the open now.*

Chapter 21

THE OTHERS

Harrison ran at the head of his party, leading the way with his long machetes sheathed on his back. He glanced upwards at the setting sun and rethought his decision to lead a party away from the safety of their walls during the most dangerous days in the lunar cycle. Three nights each moon, when it was at its fullest and the two nights either side, were the time when they huddled in fear inside their safe enclaves and hoped that the bugs didn't find a way inside.

Part of the reason why he was a war chief was because he was fearless, and he knew if he betrayed his inner fears then he might lose his position for someone younger and more reckless to take his place. He had not risen to such a position of power and influence by being reckless, but to explain that he held a very real fear of death would be to show a weakness to others. Rounding a raised knoll in the ground ahead, the walls of Three Hills loomed suddenly out of the flat ground and allowed him a well-hidden sigh of sudden relief.

The gates swung open as they approached, the sentries clearly eager not to incur his displeasure at not being alert and not recognizing him. His war party, his ten fittest and most fearless followers, jogged in behind him and stayed tall despite their aching legs and burning lungs in a display of confidence and power. Weakness was unforgivable.

Questions flew at him from the rapidly gathering crowd, all of which he ignored as he lacked the spare breath to answer any of them. Instead he walked tall and resolute through the town of randomly constructed buildings toward the central building where he finally allowed himself to fall exhausted onto a soft couch and strip off his armor and weapons.

His closest companion, and his lover more by way of position than of any other feelings, entered the room startling him, and shut the sliding door behind her. She handed him a tin cup of the fierce, distilled liquid they drank. Harrison sat up and took a swig, grimacing as the harsh drink burned down his throat to warm his empty stomach.

She watched intently as he drank before asking her question.

"Do you really think we should go back there?" she said in a low voice, just in case any prying ears were pressed to walls. "I mean, how do we know they aren't our enemies?"

"Tori," he said as he fixed her with a steely gaze, "we don't know anything. The legends speak of our people in the skies, but did you ever believe them?"

Tori cast her eyes down for a moment before fixing him again and answering, "Yes."

"So, the question remains," he went on, "are they are our enemies?"

"We could ask The Source?" she suggested carefully.

Harrison stopped with the cup halfway to his lips and regarded her, not believing what she had said.

"You want to go to war with Tanaka's people over this? You want to fight The Keepers?" he asked quietly. "You know they would have seen the others coming down from the sky just as we did."

"I think it is worth it," Tori said after a pause, flicking a dark dreadlock out of her eyeline as she stared at him.

Harrison lay back with a thud onto the cushions and drank the remaining contents of his cup. Silence hung as neither of them moved.

"Let me think about it," he said. "I need to bathe."

Tori smiled and stood, unclasping her own armor and dropping it at her feet before pulling off her top to reveal her hard, upper body and the visible scars which only made her more attractive to Harrison.

"Want company?"

The following morning, roused at the fast-breaking dawn by one of the multitude of chickens penned inside their walls, Harrison sat bolt upright in bed as he woke from the dream which haunted him. The same dream, which hadn't tormented him for many months, was nothing to do with the threat that roamed outside their walls in the darkness. Instead, it was caused by the origin of the scars on his chest, carved in a brutally simplistic T shape and created slowly with a rusted edge of jagged metal. His right hand clutched at his chest as his breathing slowly settled. Beside him, her bare back smooth and unblemished in stark contrast, Tori stirred and rolled her head to face the opposite side.

He threw off the covers as he rose and stalked naked toward the window which showed the flash of orange on the horizon. Downing the last of the water in a glass on a table, he poured himself more from a jug and repeated the process. He pulled on pants and boots, dressed in a ragged but clean shirt, and went outside armed only with the dagger on his belt.

As he strode though the town at dawn, only a few people were active between his home and the gates. Every one of them nodded in deference to him, some gestures he returned if he knew and respected the person, and others he ignored if the supplicant was of insufficient stature to acknowledge. That was how it had always been, when survival of the fittest was taken literally and their entire hierarchical existence was based on the concept.

Reaching the gates and climbing the steep wooden staircase to the ramparts, he was greeted silently by one of his lieutenants, Taylor, who had been left in charge when he led the war party south.

"Anything?" he asked.

"Nothing," Taylor responded as he tried to sound awake despite his tiredness at spending the night awake and on edge, "they didn't come past this time."

That had happened before, and fairly often in fact, but Harrison feared that they would have gone south to the new disruption to their territory. The reason he had been satisfied to leave contact with the others the previous day was that he was assured of their safety because of the encircling walls he had seen. Had they been unprepared, it was likely that they would have found nothing but wreckage and destruction. He was certain that they were prepared for the threat each moon brought, filling the darkest nights with terror and death, otherwise he would have been forced to make contact with them for fear that the newcomers would be wiped out. Thinking further, he realized that they had likely survived the first night by sheer luck that the swarm had avoided them, then the second because of their walls. He only hoped that they hadn't been foolish enough to open their gates whilst he slept, and that was what troubled him.

Did I make the right choice? he asked himself. *Should I have spoken to them and told them of the dangers?*

No, he was sure he was right to avoid them until he knew more, and was certain that they weren't like others who would kill and conquer.

The only reason that Three Hills existed at all was that the cost of waging war was simply too high to either side, and the great battle which saw huge losses on both sides as well as massive destruction to his home had left a genetic memory on his people to avoid all-out conflict. That's why he fought the cold war with Tanaka's people, and why he was wary to make contact with the others who legend had said were waiting above the clouds, in the cold blackness of space, to return to the earth.

At that moment, watching the sun burst over the treetops to bathe him in sudden warmth, he knew what he should do and he knew that Tori was right; he needed answers before he could make decisions, and the risk of conflict was worth those answers to know whether the arrival of the others was a good or bad omen for his people.

"Get some rest," he told Taylor as the town below began to grow louder and busier, "we may have trouble soon."

Our eagerness to see what our trap had caught overnight was palpable as soon as we woke. Before I could ask Annie, I saw Hendricks with a finger to his earpiece and an absent look in his eye. Glancing up and seeing my interest, he pursed his lips and shook his head.

Dammit, no bugs in our bug catcher.

Well that was my first reaction, then good sense took over and I thanked my lucky stars that nothing creepy or crawly awaited my immediate attention. Rising and stretching, I put my earpiece in on my own radio and cleared my throat, as an experiment to see if Annie was always listening to everyone.

"Good morning, David," she said almost straight away, confusing me because I could still see Hendricks nodding away to himself as he listened to his own radio.

"Morning, Annie, who is Hendricks talking to?" I asked, that curious fact jumping the queue in my brain to muscle its way to the front.

"Me," she responded, making me pull a face like I'd just sat on something intimate and uncomfortable.

"What? How?" I asked, louder than I anticipated and startling the few people awake in the room.

"David," she said in a voice that echoed with some unheard sense of being caught out by a teacher, "please don't wake the others. You have caused slight increases in adrenal responses of those who heard you speak. I am able to hold several simultaneous conversations with different people with relative ease. I have not tested the full capacity of this as yet because I do not want to operate at above seventy-five percent of my memory capacity."

I was dumbstruck, and if I was being honest with myself I suddenly stopped feeling special. Annie was now more important than I was, hell, who was I kidding, she'd always been more important than me to all this. As I was struggling to find my place in the world she spoke to me again.

"No test subject has been captured overnight," she told me, "all sensor data indicated that the anomaly did not come within detectable range of the compound."

"So, no bugs?" I said softly as I approached Hendricks and the coffee station he was guarding. Reaching him, he poured another and added a dash of sugar before handing it to me wordlessly. I nodded my thanks and poured in a splash of milk before giving it a lazy stir. As I looked up to Hendricks again, Annie patched us both in to the same conversation.

"Gentlemen," she said, "I would recommend that we continue with the internal process of constructing the base as I send scout drones further afield." She paused sufficiently to allow either of us to object if we wished. Looking at Hendricks I guessed that his coffee wasn't the first of the morning and was probably more like the last in a steady stream of caffeine which kept him going through the night.

"Medical personnel are intending to revive Engineer Mike Evans today, a matter in which I have some personal interest. I would like to devote a significant portion of my available memory to that procedure which will render me less than optimal for any tactical activity," she finished.

Realizing that my creation was displaying concern over the outcome of her actions taken in what she believed were the best interests of a human life sobered me a little. Hendricks responded before I could think of what to say.

"Of course, let me know when the procedure is due to commence and we will take over the defenses."

"Thank you," she said with an inflection I was sure I hadn't programmed.

Was that relief? Gratitude?

Shrugging it away, I asked her what I could do to be helpful, seeing as my job was as irrelevant as I could possibly imagine at that point.

"Dr. Whitmore has voiced an opinion that assistance in resuscitating those still in cryostasis would be of benefit," she told me.

"Roger that," I said as I took a sip of my coffee and pulled another face as it was too milky, and I cursed my own lack of precision before a thought struck me. "Wait, Annie?"

My earpiece chimed once which translated in my head as, "Yes?"

"Did Elliot say that to you specifically?" I asked, worried that she may be overstepping one of the unwritten rules of society.

"Negative, he was alone when he said that, would you like to hear a transcript of his words in case I misunderstood?"

"God, no, Annie!" I hissed with my head inclined down toward my radio. "You can't do that."

I glanced at Hendricks for support, but his raised eyebrows over the lip of his coffee cup told me I was on my own.

"Annie, you can't eavesdrop and then tell people what someone else has said," I admonished her gently. Hendricks cleared his throat, making me look at him.

"Possibly me at fault here, my friend," he said with such apologetic politeness that I was powerless to be angry. "I have asked Annie to monitor the population for security reasons, just in case anyone wanted to leave the compound without proper protection ..." He trailed away, leaving his eye contact with me to do the rest. I sighed and deflated.

"Fine. Annie?" I said, waiting for her response and receiving only a clipped chime as though she was sulking.

"Monitor people for safety reasons, but nobody wants to see you as Big Brother, you understand?" The earpiece chimed a double-tone to indicate that she was working, or as even she now called it, *thinking*.

"My research indicates that you are referring to this in the Orwellian fictional sense and not of the popular television program?"

"Yes, please don't tell people that you have them under constant surveillance, nobody will ever use the bathroom again ..."

Again, the tones indicated that Annie was searching her archives for information allowing her to formulate a response. I rubbed my eyes with my free hand as I regretted my decision to allow her to download the internet to her servers.

"Annie, just promise me you won't do that again unless it's important?" I asked tiredly.

"Okay, if I may, you could suggest the offer of assistance to Dr. Whitmore as your own idea?"

"Yeah, I was thinking that ..." I said lamely.

Chapter 22

THE SOURCE

Harrison selected his fiercest followers, and a few of the others who weren't part of his inner circle. The object of bringing those with him was twofold; they would see how fearless a leader he was, and they would hopefully see his skill as a warrior so would be less inclined to make or support any challenge for his leadership.

The Source was only five miles away, but that five miles took them into Tanaka's territory and any incursion would be seen as an act of aggression which would endanger the peace treaty the two factions had signed before Harrison was born. He made his way stealthily, yet still progressed his team at a good pace to cover the distance quickly.

Reaching the edge of the clearing where the trees gave way to scrub grass, he dropped to one knee in the shadows and waited, watching the sloping entrance to the underground caverns that he had never seen. The stories of the metal-walled caves were handed down between the generations, no doubt being distorted ever so slightly every time they were retold. His mind wandered to the stories of the others, of the people who fled to the heavens to escape the impacts, and wondered what distortion of their tale would be discovered soon.

One thing at a time, he told himself, focusing on the problem at hand.

Seeing no movement after ten muscle-cramping minutes of silent watching, he rose gently and indicated for five of his party to remain outside as the others followed him toward the dark maw leading below ground.

Drawing one of the dull metal blades over his right shoulder, dull except for the bright strip where the sharpening stone had left a wicked edge on the weapons, he descended into darkness and slipped a hand into a pocket to draw out one of the ancient talismans of his people. Holding the chunky wristband ahead of him as though it could ward away the evil spirits he feared lurked below the surface, a slight noise to his right made him freeze and stiffen.

No sooner had the noise bounced from his ears to his brain and down to his muscles, did another sound erupt and force him to react. The guttural scream of rage echoed in the small, cavernous space, making him throw up his weapon in desperate reply. Blades clashed, sparking brightly in the dim light, and Harrison was forced backwards by the force of the impact just as Tori let out her own cry of rage and launched into the gap he had vacated. Harrison scrambled to his feet, just as more sounds erupted in the direction of the daylight behind them as the watchers he had left behind fell on The Keepers who had emerged to descend on his invading force. Looking back, he saw that Tori had bested the wild-haired Keeper who had fallen on him without warning. He saw her own blades flash as they plunged into the neck of the man rapidly, coming out wet and dark in the low light.

Looking back to his front he saw a big man emerge from the shadows, brandishing an evil-looking axe in each hand and flicking his head to remove an errant strand of lank, dirty hair from his face. Baring his broken and blackened teeth at Harrison, the wild-eyed beast strode purposefully forward as he began to twirl both axes.

Something about the way he flourished the weapons struck fear into Harrison's heart; it wasn't for show, wasn't a demonstration of skill, but a utilitarian movement designed only to prepare for battle. Harrison dropped the wristband into the dirt and drew the other machete from over his left shoulder. Twirling both blades in his own approximation of the spinning axes to pup precious blood into his arms, he threw himself into the fight.

Meeting the attack head-on as fast as he could, Harrison saw the outcome long before it happened. He saw the two axe heads singing through the air to meet in the middle right where his head joined his body, and he knew with utter certainty what the result of walking into that blow would mean. He saw further, knowing that this attacker left unchecked in the rear of their group would cut a murderous path through toward the daylight, and would likely spell the death of them all.

Knowing all of this in a heartbeat, he still threw himself forward.

Dropping to his knees and allowing the small impetus of his short charge to carry him under the decapitating double swing, he slashed viciously with his right, then his left hand, opening up the exposed belly of the man to spill hot, wet intestines onto the dirt before him. The sudden shock and pain of the attack rendered the wild man instantly useless and dropped him to his knees to allow Harrison to stand and line up his fatal blow which split the skull in one savage downward strike. Using his boot to free the blade, he turned to watch as Tori had finally finished stabbing his initial attacker in the neck so many times that the head was half severed.

Looking further back, he saw that only one of The Keepers still lived but was now hopelessly outnumbered and cornered.

"Hold!" he snapped, preventing one of his warriors from stepping forward to skewer the creature through the stomach. The spear tip stopped, quavering a hand's breadth from the soft target. Eyes switching wildly between the half circle of invaders, the face streaked with rivulets of tears running through the dirt, the final surviving Keeper locked eyes with Harrison as he had spoken to save its life.

Realizing that this one was different, Harrison stepped forward to look at it closer. It was younger than the others, cleaner in a way with hints of un-matted hair. He returned the stare and came to an instant decision. Saying nothing, he stepped forward and punched the hilt of his machete into the side of its head, knocking it cold. Stepping back to watch the small body slump to the ground, Harrison ordered the unconscious body to be watched, then returned to the body of the first Keeper he had slain and kicked around in the wet mess of dirt and guts to find the wristband he had been forced to drop.

He found it and ripped a strip of cloth from one of the bodies to wipe it clean, then began again to descend down the long tunnel into the blackness below.

Eventually, the oppressive darkness of the underground tunnel fighting against the harsh, bright light of the torch Tori held aloft, stopped suddenly at a circular metal door. No obvious mechanism to open it was visible, and Harrison sheathed his weapon and slipped the sticky wristband over his hand, fighting down the shudder of disgust in case it was seen as a sign of weakness.

A low hum sounded from seemingly within the door, before lights blinked into existence and a hiss sounded. The door rolled open, surging a wash of colder air past them as it fought its way through the gap into the warm air as nature sought to redress the balance of difference. Stepping forward over the threshold without hesitation, Harrison was the first man to step inside the facility in a generation. Everywhere he walked, lights flashed into life and sounds of machinery and systems powering up filled the air.

Standing still in the center of a large room he dropped his hands to his sides and spoke loudly.

"Hello?"

A dull beep sounded loudly, echoing around the space as it seemed to come from everywhere and nowhere at once.

"Hello," came the distorted, synthesized answer in an approximation of a woman's voice, making the small crowd of others hiss excitedly to one another. Harrison closed his eyes to temper himself. He had just started a war for the uncertain chance to have questions answered, and he had passed the first two hurdles without encountering failure. He only hoped that what happened next would make the risk worth it.

"Can you tell me about the others?" he intoned in what he hoped was a strong voice. "About the others in space?"

A double chime sounded before the voice burst back over the speakers once more, the words fractured and distorted.

"Sierra f-facility," it started, "was a sur-r-rvival project utilizing the acquired Intern-n-national Space Station-n-n. T-two hundred a-a-and ninet-t-teen people were c-c-cryogenically stored at t-t-the fa-cility-t-ty."

"When?"

"The facility was active pr-r-rior to the impa-a-act in twenty-y-y-thirty-three."

Another two hundred people? From hundreds of years ago?

"Can you contact them?" he asked.

"Neg-g-gative. Authoriza-a-ation required."

"Who's authorization?" Harrison intoned, fearing the answer.

"Error, you a-a-are not authorized."

"What else is here, in this place?" he asked, changing the subject and hearing the response tone warble as it crackled through the air.

"A-a-all supplies and st-t-torage have been removed, only-y-y power supply remains."

Harrison thought about this response. Somehow, hearing a confirmation of what he believed to be true about their lives was both satisfying and devastating; as though the loss of knowledge that there was anything else out there crushed his inner child.

"Have you told anyone that we are here?" he asked.

"Com-m-munications with other faci-i-ilities are non-functioning," the voice told him.

Good, he thought, *at least Tanaka won't find out about The Keepers for a while.*

Turning back toward the doorway, seeing that the others had only just begun to step tentatively inside, he called out his orders.

"Tori, get those bodies dragged into the woods and cover up as much as possible," he instructed, and saw her give the orders to others before he turned his attention back to The Source.

"Are they ... good?" he asked tentatively, uncertainly, more quietly.

No response came, making him fear that the tortured sounding voice had gone away forever.

"Hey!" he snapped, louder. Hearing the strangled tone reverberate back to him he let out his breath in relief.

"To activate v-v-voice inter-rface, say, Annie," the voice answered.

"Annie?" Harrison said, not out of following the instructions but in confusion that The Source he had heard legends about had a name. A chime sounded, wavering as the noise bounced around the empty air. Belatedly he recognized that the noise was an acknowledgement to him speaking, and he tried again.

"Annie, are the people from space good?"

"Error, please r-r-rephrase the question," the voice responded.

"Annie, who was on the facility in space?"

"Error, you a-a-are not authorized."

Exasperated, Harrison abandoned the malfunctioning Source of legend, having revealed it to be nothing but a damaged and barely functioning computer system.

After years of wary peace based on the concept of mutually assured destruction, Harrison had to face the prospect of war with Tanaka's people, as well as the decision of how to deal with the newcomers.

Friend or foe, he asked himself, *friend or foe.*

~

The ragged woman ran through the jungle, stumbling over the uneven ground in her panic as she lost her footing. Breathing raggedly, her rearward glances served only to blind her to the perilous footing and heighten her fear that the invaders were hot on her heels in pursuit.

She had been at the very edge of the trees when the first warriors crept stealthily forward. She went to rise but was held back by the silent gesture from the bigger man to her right as he shot out a flat palm, telling her to wait. The seconds ticked by in slow time, each heartbeat an agonizing eternity until their whole group sprang forward to follow them into the tunnel entrance and fall on their unprotected rear. She jumped up to follow, but instead of finding her feet she tangled herself on a slippery tree root and fell back down. By the time she had regained her feet she froze in horror as others emerged from the cover of the trees to attack the ambushers. Her fear kept her there, even as the cries and wet sounds of weapons striking flesh echoed out to her senses. Powerless to act, she instead turned and fled to raise the alarm.

Eventually finding the safety of the walls, she ignored the shout of warning from the sentry and fell on the gates to hammer her dirty fists on the metal. The entrance creaked open as she stood with her hands on her knees trying to regain her breath, and she stood to stagger inside where the fearsome leader was framed motionless by an armed entourage.

"The Source," she cried, "has been attacked."

The Tanaka, the seventeenth leader of the town, kept his face stern and unimpressed, suppressing the savage and violent anger he felt inside.

Turning away from her he gestured to two men stood nearby, and they stepped forward to seize her arms roughly and drag her inside as the gates behind her closed.

Chapter 23

NEW BEGINNINGS

Life inside the ring of metal that protected the returning citizens of Earth began to take on more of an everyday feel. Each morning more people were revived and brought up to speed with their situation. Some took it well, others less so. Some knew or had worked with people who were based in the other sites, and despite the certain knowledge that everything was *un*certain when they went under, they still had emotions to deal with. Everyone mourned the loss of the world in their own way, and some showed it more openly than others.

Catarina, alive in her element and finding her expertise in almost constant need, spent more time in her primary profession as she helped the survivors cope with the complex and conflicting emotions they felt. Survivors guilt was what most people experienced, some more intensely than others as they had been forced to choose a limited number of people to join them. That had been one of the main reasons that those selected from the plethora of people with the specialist skills desired had been selected: for their lack of immediate family. Most were single men and women with little or no relatives, but still the sight of the first children walking around with their parents tugged at everyone's feelings.

A pharmaceutical solution was utilized to get the worst affected through the initial difficult period, and that required diagnosis and monitoring by psychiatric specialists.

Since the second night on the planet, there had been no sign of the small swarm that had encircled the small preserve and that fact gave some comfort where others were experiencing a sense of impending trouble. The engineering teams had branched out from the ring of pods under the protection of the team members and had begun to clear wide swathes of the jungle. They stripped and piled the straight trunks of the new variant of palms and kept their rubbery branches and leaves separate. Those long lengths of straight timber were split and left to dry ready for use in construction and the cleared land was ploughed using the precious few electrically powered all-terrain vehicles. Their immediate surroundings were explored, always under armed protection, and samples of earth, foliage, and the few species of animal life that were encountered were all rigorously tested by the growing team of scientists.

Every single person had a purpose, a list of daily tasks regardless of age but geared to their own individual strengths. Children worked in the kitchens and attended afternoon education in one of the masses of hard-wearing shelters erected inside the walls. Hendricks spent as much time as he could near there without ignoring his primary duties, as his wife was the teacher and his daughter attended the classes.

Another familiar sight to everyone there was the severe and serious Hayley Cole, who appeared without warning all over their compound bearing a heavy-duty clipboard and with a tablet computer slung across her body like a purse. She always smiled, but that smile was part of her corporate training as though she had attended seminars on how to make people work more effectively.

She had, and part of the reason she was so effective in her chosen field was because she had an uncanny knack for motivating people to do something, believing that it was actually their idea in the first place.

A week in, their progress was halted by a sudden and violent downpour as though the heavens simply emptied in one go. People ran for cover, laughing and shrieking at their unexpected soaking, whereas their meteorologist stood looking skyward and ignored the heavy rain.

William Tremblay, heavy set and African American in appearance, had formerly been Canada's foremost expert on weather systems. Having left his birth country for college and never returning for more than the briefest of visits, he had lived and worked in Miami at the National Hurricane Center where he had been involved in a decade-long study of the four most accurate hurricane prediction methods. A quiet man inclined toward his own company, Tremblay just stared up as his lips moved silently. He was counting to sixty, letting the seconds tick off in his mind to see if the sudden rainfall was like many of the tropical downpours he had experienced. After a minute passed, he looked down and removed his glasses to pointlessly wipe them clear of water, an air of disappointment surrounding him as he trudged toward shelter.

I ran inside, wishing I could strip off my shirt that was clinging to me like I'd worn it in the shower. I had, in a way, but my discomfort was heavily outweighed by my insecurity as I glanced up to see Stevens and Weber already ahead of my idea. Seeing two professional soldiers, both strong and heavily muscled with a body fat percentage far lower than my own, shirtless and scanning my eyes to the surreptitious glances of the women in sight, I decided not to embarrass myself. Satisfying the partial need to dry out, I made do by squeezing out the loose material and wringing the warm water out onto the ground.

The air inside the shelter soon became thick and sweaty with so many wet bodies seeking respite and people laughed with one another. As one, a select number of people suddenly snapped-to and concentrated into the earpieces a lot of us wore as there were many sets of ears listening now.

For some reason, probably out of Annie's loyalty I imagined, I was included in this select few.

"Contact detected," she said in hushed tones as though she was trying to keep her voice down, "tree line, two hundred meters, I'm reading one of the Charlie site personnel."

A pause followed as Hendricks, Me, Weber, and Stevens all exchanged glances; our faces betrayed that we had all been included in the information. Without the fuss or flurry of movement, the three team members quietly collected their gear and made their way toward the exit at a walk. I followed them, forcing myself not to react and ask questions that could cause panic. The others jogged toward the gate, the rest of the team coming from different directions having been given the unexpected news. Amir was there, rapidly getting soaked as he had been in the dry when the rain started, and Hendricks was the first to hit his radio.

"Private channel?" he asked, hearing a rapid chime from Annie to signal the affirmative.

"How do you know?" I asked, not bothering to press the button on the radio as I knew she would be listening to our mics.

"Wristband," she responded immediately, "functionality is limited but I am receiving intermittent vital signs data from the device. It belongs to a Milstone, Dr. Robert E."

"Can you speak to them?" Magda asked, seeking a way to make contact without risking a confrontation.

"Negative, there are no speakers or microphones in range."

"Can you get a drone to them?" Amir asked. "Maybe use that?"

"Negative, drones unable to fly due to adverse weather conditions."

"We go then," Hendricks said as he checked his weapon and watched as his team stacked up in a line behind him, a hand on the shoulder of the one on front. "Annie, can you give us directions to them and call out any changes?"

Again, the single, streamlined chime of affirmation came through our earpieces.

With a nod, Hendricks opened the gate wide enough to get through and led the way. His team fanned out either side of him so that they proceeded in a ragged line spaced far enough apart that any attack should not be able to encompass them all.

"I guess we wait here?" I said, looking at Amir who nodded and drew his sidearm to hold it down toward the ground. I did the same, watching as the team disappeared into the steaming mist brought on by the rainfall onto hot ground.

"One hundred meters," Annie said in a low voice to Hendricks, "raised ground, turn twelve degrees right."

"Roger," Hendricks whispered, instead turning a few degrees left to avoid a head-on approach. He heard the double chime in his ear to indicate that Annie was calculating, then the down tone to signify that she had stopped the interaction.

What Annie had done, was to call up the training manual produced for the three security teams which had been used to assess a candidate's tactical ability. She quickly, in a microsecond in fact, cross-referenced the situation with the training and surmised that Hendricks was leading his team on an encircling maneuver to approach the target from the rear and effectively cut off their escape. Assessing this in an instant, she discarded the voice interaction she had loaded for use to ask why he was deviating from the instructions, and instead said nothing.

She understood that there were things she didn't yet know, and even more things that she couldn't yet do.

"Forty meters to your right now," she updated, hearing no response and waiting.

"It's moving," she said in a louder, more urgent tone, "heading directly toward you."

Hendricks hissed for the attention of his team and held aloft his left hand as his eye was still to the optic of the assault rifle tucked hard into his right shoulder. The rest of the team fanned out, some taking cover behind trees as Hendricks stood resolutely in his firing pose to face the unknown.

A snap of a tree branch to their left made their heads turn just as Annie's voice whispered in his ear.

"Fifteen meters, you should have acquired the target visually by n—"

"Stop!" Hendricks barked loudly, as movement to his front showed. "Identify yourself!"

Silence.

"Identify yourself," he said again, dropping his voice lower and investing a hint of menace to his words. He had so often experienced this and knew that commands given in a tone of voice that left absolutely no illusion that you were to be fucked with, inevitably meant that you wouldn't have to resort to firing your weapon.

Slowly, a shape melted out of the heavy foliage and walked toward him with both hands held aloft.

Hendricks straightened slightly, his shock unmistakable as he was clearly not looking at a scientist fresh out of cryo. Instead, he saw a tall, lean young man with evident equal measures of strength and grace in his movements, much as the way a professional soldier carried himself. He wore two long knives, or short swords depending on how you looked at it, strapped on his back and his dirty, scarred face spoke of a mind which was much older than he looked. He seemed to be about twenty-five, still a kid in so many ways, but the eyes were flint-hard and edgy, as though the kid wasn't a kid at all, and had seen things that would turn a person's hair white.

"I said," Hendricks went on in his most commanding voice, "identify yourself."

The young man sighed and still said nothing. Hendricks flicked his eyes sideways to see Jones, their former UK special forces frogman, and nodded him forward. Jones let his rifle drop on its sling and covered the distance in six confident strides where he ran his hands over the young man before drawing the two machetes to disarm him. The kid looked directly at Hendricks and smiled, before letting out a short, sharp whistle.

Around them, the jungle came alive as others emerged from the foliage to point weapons at them. Jones reacted first, kicking his captive in the backs of his knees to force him to the ground before placing the business edge of one his seized blades to the side of his neck, then crouched down behind him. All around were shouts of warning and threat as the team members bawled out commands for weapons to be dropped.

"Enough," the man on his knees called out tiredly.

"We are not your enemy," he said as he fixed Hendricks' gaze once more, "but we do not know if you are ours yet."

With that, he ducked his head away from the blade and came up on the other side to force his body weight backwards and rise up before the other ones could. Drawing another blade which had been missed on the quick search he pointed it toward the Brit and glanced at Hendricks, guessing him to be the shot caller, and suddenly reversed the dagger by spinning it in the air and catching the tip to offer it as surrender.

Hendricks lowered his rifle and stood tall, seeing that he was only an inch or two taller than the younger man.

"You're clearly not Dr. Milstone," Hendricks said as he stepped closer, "so who the hell are you?"

"Annie, have you got everyone we need on the channel?" Hendricks' voice came through my earpiece.

"Yes," Annie responded, "key personnel are tuned in. Do you want me to list the people on this channel?"

"No, that's fine," Hendricks responded, the sound of talking and moving over rough ground translating through his works on the radio. "Okay, listen up, we are bringing two people back to the base. They are not openly hostile but we don't fully understand each other just yet, shall we say. Recommend we bring the meeting outside instead. Anyone disagree?"

Silence was his only answer, like a kind of non-verbal tumbleweed. Amir called up to acknowledge and to say that he was on his way.

I joined the small group about fifty meters away under the barely adequate cover of the thickest copse of trees to shelter from the rain. As I got there I took in the sight of the young man and woman who were as similar as possible to us, only so far away from who we were. I knew that these people must have been born here—I knew because Annie had caught me up privately on my short walk to the gate—and that made them all over nine hundred years younger than us. Basically, we came from a different time, a different world, from these two. We were like time travelers from the future, only we came from the past and left a legacy which seemed to have sent humanity back in time. By the time I had joined them my head hurt from the quantum mechanics of my explanation to myself, and I was soaked to the skin again.

"Hi," I said, holding up one flat hand in an awkward and un-natural gesture which seemed to me to be somewhere between a high-five I chickened out of and an old-fashioned German military salute that was just not polite to make. The two just stared back at me, so I didn't try again and just kept my socially inept mouth shut.

One by one, a small handful of others joined us, and Annie an-nounced simply that we were all here.

"On behalf of this settlement, I would like to exten—" Amir began until Harrison pointedly turned away and spoke to Hendricks.

"Why is he speaking?" he asked simply, his eyebrows pointing upwards as they almost met over the bridge of his nose.

Hendricks looked to Amir and shrugged, so Amir answered the question.

"I am the one who put all of this together," he began haughtily. "I organized and funded all of the projects. If it wasn't for me then none of us would be standing here, and you wouldn't be alive."

Harrison looked at him wearing the same incredulous facial ex-pression, then back to Hendricks.

"He should not speak like that," he said carefully, "it is seen as a challenge to your leadership. You should confront his challenge," he explained helpfully. Hendricks chuckled and gave Amir an apol-ogetic smile.

"Harrison," he said seriously but still wearing most of the smile, "we obviously have a different way of working than you do. We all have different roles, and, well, we are the warriors if you like, whereas others—"

"What do you do?" Harrison asked Amir suddenly as he turned to face him, "are you a warrior too?"

"No, I'm a ..." Amir started to answer. "... I'm a, I *was*, the CEO. And a lawyer ..."

Harrison looked back to Hendricks, a pleading look of confusion on his face.

"It doesn't matter," Hendricks said aloud to sweep away the awkwardness. "Moving on, everyone, this is Harrison and Tori. They are from a place called Three Hills."

"Situated ten-point-six miles north by north-east from our location. The route on foot is half as long again as a river crossing is necessary and no bridges or roads have been constructed in this direction," Annie reported via the speakers and earpieces of the group's radios.

Harrison's eyes went wide on hearing the voice, so I decided I should say something at that point.

"That's Annie," I told them as I tapped a finger on my radio, "she kinda runs things around here, but you know, the computer stuff anyways ..." Realizing I'd probably just made things worse, I looked around for help but everyone else was watching them as they bent their heads together and whispered.

"I have heard this voice before," Harrison said as he stepped too close to me and looked at my radio. I stiffened, and I was the first to admit that I was more than a little scared at that point.

"Harrison, Tori, greetings," Annie said in a soft tone as though she was suddenly a navigation system giving voice commands to a stressed-out male driver. "I presume from your possession of the wristband and your recognition of my vocal patterns, that you have interfaced with the ANII system at site Charlie?"

Harrison looked back to Hendricks again, waiting for a translation from a fellow warrior.

"Did you go underground into a big place and talk to the same voice?" he asked with blunt simplicity. Harrison smiled.

"Yes. It is called The Source, but it doesn't work. Not like your Source who makes sense. Mostly," he finished with a smirk.

"That system you interfaced with," Annie picked up, having analyzed and streamlined her interaction protocols with Harrison, "is like I used to be, but has probably malfunctioned over the time it has been active here. It was made to interact with the people who wore those bands," she said, then obviously replayed the interaction as she analyzed her interaction protocols before adding, "the source you spoke to is broken, but I'm different."

Harrison nodded his understanding sagely.

Now that bit was weird. Only for me because, well I must be a little weird, but maybe I was the only one to imagine our invisible, un-bodied and now-sentient computer nod her head toward the dull thing around his right wrist. He looked at it, then back up at Hendricks who showed him his own. In contrast, Hendricks' was shiny and flashed little LED pin-pricks of light if you lifted it up, whereas the one Harrison wore looked, well it looked about a thousand years old is what it looked like.

"So …" Harrison started, his brain spinning to catch up. "Source Annie?"

"You may call me Annie, it's quicker that way," she said.

"The other Source isn't like yours," he said to Hendricks as he returned to the most comfortable default in the conversation.

"That's because the *other Source*," Annie said acidly in yet another voice pattern derivative I didn't program, "isn't like me because only *I* am like me."

That shut everyone up. Already everyone inside the ring of space pods had accustomed quickly to Annie being a *her* and not an *it,* but Harrison obviously wasn't copied in on that email.

"Anyway," Hendricks said in gentle interruption, "perhaps we had better start from the beginning? Harrison, you obviously came here to talk, yes?"

He nodded.

"So, how can we help you?"

"I want your help to overthrow Tanaka," he answered simply.

I'll admit, I was the first to drop my jaw and start throwing looks around the group as though I didn't understand a damn thing about how any of this made sense.

Chapter 24

THE TANAKA

It took me all of about ten seconds to realize that the guy wasn't talking about Tanaka, at least not the same irritating asshole I remembered from his visits to Texas, but his direct descendants. I listened intently as Harrison told their history as it had been told to him, and it made for an interesting bedtime story. Frightening, but interesting.

Tanaka had been the first to break out from their underground transport into the future, and he had controlled everything. He had first settled Three Hills and forced the first travelers, as they referred to those who went into cryo, to work and build his empire. He had grown the settlement and driven a thriving community under the constant threat of punishment, imprisonment, and what amounted to torture for anyone who spoke out against him and his soldiers. They had great weapons which could kill instantly, much like the ones Hendricks' team held low or let hang on their slings, and they dominated.

Tanaka decided that Three Hills wasn't enough, and he pushed his scouts out further north and east to settle other camps and begin to grow them too. The first of these was on a site where hot water bubbled up out of the ground, and, imaginatively, he called it Hot

Springs. Tanaka moved himself and his followers there and ruled for two hundred years until he handed down the leadership to one of his descendants.

"Wait," Stevens interrupted holding up a hand, "hold up. He ruled for two hundred years? The guy was, what? Forty when he went in? You telling me this guy lived for almost two hundred and fifty years? Anyone else?"

As he spoke, those who hadn't already connected the dots did so.

"Tanaka," Amir said with his forefinger and thumb scratching the stubble on his chin, "did he disappear for long periods of time only to come back?"

"Yes," Harrison answered with an amused smile.

"And it was the same guy?"

"He claimed to be, but they believed it was another man claiming to be him. Why?"

"Just a guess. Please, continue."

Tanaka ruled from his throne in Hot Springs, delegating squads of soldiers to ensure the compliance of the other settlements, both large and small. Food and supplies were sent to their leader, as were children and young people who were required to enter into long contracts of servitude. After years of this, when the first travelers had all gone and were replaced by their children's, children's, children, an uprising began in Three Hills and sparked a war. The timing of the uprising had coincided with one of Tanaka's longer periods of absence from the public eye, and he returned in time to lead the battle to quell the main body of rebels in their first settlement.

This civil war, as small scale and brief as it was, wrought a destruction on the settlements and almost left Three Hills burnt to the ground before peace was agreed. After that, years of oppression reigned until Tanaka finally handed down control to another of his name, a great-great grandson perhaps, and normality returned.

For a while at least, because their war and the huge inferno had attracted the attention of something devastating and unexpected.

"It is called The Swarm," Harrison said, his eyes wandering upwards as he spoke of the terrifying things in the dark, "and it comes each moon when it is at its darkest and no light casts onto the earth. They have come at other times, according to legend, but never in the light."

"What are they?" I blurted out, not even certain that I knew I was going to speak until it happened.

"The Swarm? They are large insects, like the ants in the jungles and the beetles in the leaf dirt. They strip anything in their path clean; I've seen entire bodies of men cleaned down to dry bones in minutes," he said, with an almost passionate glee at the frightening violence. "If they find a wall high enough and nothing attracts their attention, they simply carry on without bothering us, and that is how we have lived for generations. We are at peace with the others, because any of us could so easily bring death to people by damaging their walls and letting The Swarm do the rest. It is what the legends call mutually assured destruction."

Eyes met knowingly among our group. The world had ended, the planet had changed, a thousand years had passed and still the concept of humans eradicating one another endured.

"Do you know how Tanaka executes people?" Tori stepped in to ask. A few shakes of heads answered her question.

"He has them stripped naked and staked to the ground for The Swarm to devour them," she finished, leaving a silence which stretched until another voice spoke.

"So," said Jones, shocking people by speaking out loud when he usually kept everything to himself, "we've gone and pitched our bloody tents in the middle of a cold war with killer insects on the loose?"

"Looks that way," I said, half in shock. I cast my eyes up to the others; some quiet in their own thoughts, a few scanning the tree line out of defensive habit, and some staring at Harrison and Tori in the hope that they had better news. Amir perked up first, returning to a subject he still hadn't fully understood.

"So," he said with a furrowed brow, "is the first Tanaka still alive?"

"The first?" Tori answered, shooting an almost embarrassed look at Harrison. "Of course not, how could he be?"

It was Amir's turn to glance to his people for support, and Hendricks bailed him out.

"What do you know about the very beginning?" he asked. "About how we survived the asteroid?"

Harrison's uneasy look told him that he didn't know much, or at least he was wary of saying what he believed in front of people who would know more of the truth than he suspected he did. He wasn't a leader because he was quick to demonstrate a lack of knowledge.

"Only that our ancestors went underground …"

"Yes, into a facility controlled by another Annie, but do you know how they lived for so long there?" Hendricks asked carefully, receiving a shake of Harrison's head.

"We all went into something called cryostasis, those who went underground as well as us in space," he said, raising an unnecessary finger toward the sky to unconsciously make his point, "and that kept us in a sleep-like state where our bodies didn't age. I think that is how the first Tanaka stayed alive for so long; he went in and out of cryostasis for years at a time before coming back out to give orders."

Harrison and Tori exchanged a look. One which was both disbelieving and simultaneously seemed as though the distance between their beliefs and the facts had suddenly been shortened.

"So," Nathalie said, changing the subject, "why do you need our help with this Tanaka, and what are you proposing?"

Harrison seemed to swell as he drew in a breath and straightened up to fix Hendricks with a resolute stare.

"The cycle needs to be broken. My ancestors have tried to unite our people and find the source of The Swarm, but Tanaka will not combine forces. He thinks we are beneath him. They are warlords, and I fear that our peace cannot last. We have to be decisive, and with your help"—he gestured toward their weapons—"we can finally turn the tide."

Our group exchanged looks until Hendricks took the lead, primarily, I thought, to ward off the words which would come from Amir's mouth.

"We need to talk about this," he said, to close off the conversation, "will you come back in a few days to discuss it?"

Harrison and Tori exchanged a look before he answered.

"The moon will soon be dropping, and we have many things to do," he said ominously. "We will return when the new moon rises in just over a week, but please," he said intently, "*do not risk contact with The Swarm.*"

I'm certain it wasn't just me who felt a sinking feeling of cold as we walked back to the ring of pods, which didn't look anywhere near tall enough for my liking.

Chapter 25

BREAKING THE NEWS

Assembling the survivors from space to fill them in on the newly learned facts, the duty seemed to fall to Hendricks, as Amir's confidence and flair for public speaking seemed to have abandoned him. Mindful not to lay it out as brutally as Jones did, he waited patiently until the group, which now neared almost seventy-five, gathered near the center of their enclave and forced him to climb up on one of the three pods there to be seen by everyone.

He started with the expected revelation that we were not alone on the planet, but then hushed the excited buzz of the crowd by warning them that things here weren't as we expected.

"We have landed in the middle of some feudal or tribal power struggle," he said, "because it has been so long since the others came out of cryo we are now in possession of the dominant technology, and we are going to have to find a way of making peace or choosing a side …" He was forced to stop speaking as the noise rising from the crowd drowned out his voice. He held up both hands and called out for quiet, waiting as the rumble lowered.

"That's not all," he went on, a dark look on his face, "in our absence, another species has emerged on the planet; we don't know what, nor do we understand anything about it without scientific study, but *nobody* is to leave the compound during darkness. Now, we all have tasks, please can we all return to them."

He lowered himself and jumped lightly down and walked back toward the cluster of people who had been outside the walls. Unbidden, they huddled in around him, all but the most astute of them ignorant of the power shift that had just subtly taken place. It had started when Harrison spoke to Hendricks as he was the leader of the soldiers, and his inability to comprehend that they would answer to, or follow, a man like Amir who was clearly no warrior was beyond his acceptance.

Shooting a surreptitious glance around to see if they were being overheard, he asked the group for their suggestions. Some were in favor of closing up the compound tight and letting the conflict outside draw its own conclusion, others were in support of joining the fight.

"On my third tour of Afghanistan," Willard Stevens said in quiet thought, "our unit was approached by a local fighter who asked for our help. He said he needed the American soldiers to help him fight a war lord who fought against our 'occupation.' This guy had grade-A intel and led us in easily. We took the base out without any losses, then reported back to HQ only to find out that we'd just taken out a friendly group. The guy who came to us was Taliban, and we got played."

"Your point?" Magda asked him, her soft voice removing any harshness in her words.

"My point?" Stevens said with a wan smile. "Is that the story we've just been fed sounds bad; like, bad enough that our consciences are telling us to take this other guy out. How many sides to a coin?"

"Agreed," Weber said, "we cannot act on this intelligence without corroborations."

Nods rippled around the group as an agreement not to get involved without more information. Realizing that he hadn't heard from the biggest brain there, Hendricks said aloud, "Annie, anything to add?"

A second's pause, before her hurried voice came over our radios.

"Standby one," she said in a clipped tone, making us all exchange confused looks. A second later, the soft chime indicated that she was back with us.

"Sorry, I was calculating and had to use most of my available memory, so I just replayed the sensory feed from all sources to analyze the data," she explained enigmatically.

"And?" Anderson prompted, more out of interest in her processes than the facts.

"And I am now up to speed," she responded quickly. "Hendricks, my thoughts are in agreement. I have reviewed the orbital footage of the area and calculated that Harrison's story matches what I witnessed from space, within expected parameters for anecdotal inaccuracy. I cannot hypothesize on whether this Tanaka is likely to be a better choice of ally or not, but if I were able to connect to the system at the site which Harrison referred to as The Source, then I could interrogate that system for factual answers and not legends passed down through generations."

"So, your recommendations?" Hendricks asked.

"My recommendations are prioritized," she answered, a slight and subtle change in her voice as though there were the smallest hint of a question in her words. "First priority is to capture test subjects from *The Swarm*"—she invested the words with the dramatic gravitas that Harrison had used—"and find a way to neutralize that threat."

"Are you ..." Hendricks began hesitantly, "are you taking the piss out of Harrison?"

"A little," Annie responded in a tone of voice that made me mindful of a crooked smile on one half of the mouth she didn't possess. "How did I do?"

"Pretty well, actually," Hendricks said before recapping. "So, we lock down, catch a couple of bugs, and see how to kill them, then find out if Harrison is telling the truth about Tanaka being the bad guy and find a way that we can all get along together whilst we plug Annie into a thousand-year-old version of her former self?"

"Not necessarily in that order," Annie said, "there are other concerns and priority tasks, but I will reassess to see if they are more important than your list." She paused for a second. "Done. Negative, other tasks are not prioritized."

"What are the other tasks?" Amir asked, reminding most that the quiet businessman was still with them, after his claims of leading humanity into the future. His slow descent into obscurity as his talents were no longer that important in the new world had seemed to gather momentum over the last few days.

"Priority research on the coast," she said, reminding them that due to the continental changes, what had previously been central Africa was now the west coast where it met the much-enlarged Atlantic oceans, "as well as further studies on flora and fauna and the start of the farming programs."

"But it's more important to not get wiped out by killer ants or stumble into a war before that, right?" Anderson asked, attempting and failing to lighten the mood.

"Yes," Annie chorused, along with most of the team.

Tanaka had ordered The Keeper who had fled to the Springs, as his town name was simplified to by those who lived there, to be imprisoned and stripped of her talismans that had, according to legend, been imbued with mythical gifts of sight and strength.

Her crime had been to abandon her duties, which she accepted under a blood-oath as she was effectively married to the life-long task of protecting The Source.

Tanaka knew that, had she not fled to warn him of the attack, he would not have known about the treacherous breaking of the peace accord with Three Hills for another month almost before the supply convoy was sent to The Keepers and their absence or bodies discovered.

Still, regardless of how fortuitous the timing of her news had been, she had still broken a sacred vow and abandoned her brothers and sisters to save her own life. She had to be made an example of, and the treachery had to be punished.

He had a few days to consider how best to do both, and quickly made up his mind.

The Swarm would do both for him.

He selected a half dozen young and aspiring warriors, giving them a savage speech about how the chosen ones would be immortalized and their names would be remembered forever. He told them how their brave actions would result in the Springs finally destroying the Hills, how they would take over their resources and survivors, if there were any, and how the people of the Springs would grow in strength. He heard from all of them, choosing the three most fanatical in his mind, and took them into his grand hall to be prepared for when the moon was at its fullest as he ignored the wails of mothers outside.

Chapter 26

DECISIONS

"I still say we should put more pods out to try and catch these things," I said to the small team assembled for our priority project.

"By my calculations," said Dr. Bill Tremblay, the resident weather expert, "we still have three days before the next full moon, and even then, there's no guarantee that they will come here from what I've heard."

"Annie?" I asked, not because I didn't believe Bill who was placidly calm about the whole thing, as though science grounded him, but because I wanted a second opinion to back him up.

"I concur," Annie answered, "with both the assessment of the lunar cycle and the uncertainty of The Swarm's movements."

"Which gives us time to visit this Hot Springs place and talk," Hendricks interjected.

"I'll come with you," Amir chimed in, eager to find something to do as he seemed to fade more into obscurity every day. Hendricks nodded at him.

"At dawn then?" he asked the group. "From what Harrison told us, there's maybe thirty miles of rough ground to cover which could take us most of the day."

Agreement all round, I felt it was my responsibility to be the voice of negativity.

"And if you don't come back?" I asked carefully, silencing the group as they glanced between the assembled faces.

"I'll take myself and two of the team, and Amir, and the rest will stay here. Annie, will we have comms over that distance?"

"I've been working on that," she answered instantly, "by using drones as relays, I can piggy-back the communications network to give you coverage. I'll need you to wear cameras linked to your radios so that I can provide real-time intelligence."

"Done," Hendricks said, "anything else?"

Nobody answered, and we put back on our public faces to show that everything was okay before we rejoined the others for the evening meal. Hendricks gestured for Stevens and Geiger to join him, with Amir hovering by his side. Deciding to take advantage of my unique position, I walked away alone and muttered down to my radio.

"Annie?"

"Private channel open, how can I help, David?" she answered in a hushed tone.

"Can you open Hendricks' mic to me?" I asked conspiratorially. A double tone gave me my answer, and Hendricks' voice crackled into my earpiece.

"… get there, you two stay away from the town and keep our weapons. We go in and talk to them. Annie will tell you if we have to stay overnight, but if they are hostile then don't waste any time; just get back here."

"You sure you wanna go in unarmed, boss?" I heard Geiger's voice ask.

"I don't want to complicate anything by showing them weapons," Hendricks answered. "It'll probably be bad enough just being there with radios but I'm not going in blind. Annie? Can you keep eyes on us if a drone is out of sight of the town?"

"*Hang on,*" she whispered in my earpiece.

"Yes," she said aloud in a more authoritative voice, "effective wireless range of a drone is up to one mile. With variables in terrain and atmospherics, I should be able to link to your personal equipment without a drone being detected."

"Thanks," Hendricks answered.

"*I'm back,*" Annie whispered to me again, making me smile despite myself as she seemed to be enjoying herself playing spy.

"Okay then," Hendricks said, "at dawn. And keep this to ourselves."

With that, the radio crackled again which I took as indication that the connection was disconnected.

"David?" Annie asked, drawing out my name in a comedic voice which was both reprimanding and amused. "Wasn't it you who told me that I wasn't allowed to eavesdrop?"

"Actually," I said, intentionally making my voice peevish but still keeping it low, "I believe I told you that you shouldn't eavesdrop on people and tell others what they said ..."

She was silent for a few seconds, either thinking about her response or following a speech pattern that entailed a dramatic pause, before answering me.

"I believe that is semantics," she corrected me, "and you just broke your own rules."

"For a good reason," I told her seriously, "because I don't like this. We were supposed to land back on Earth and be happy as we rebuilt everything. Instead, we've landed in a hot jungle in the middle of a war and there are bugs. I don't like this one bit."

"Agreed," she answered, mirroring my concerned tone, "I don't like it either, but I'll be careful tomorrow."

Dawn came, and with it came a gentle chime which rose in volume until the wristbands of everyone out of cryo came awake to start the day. Water was heated, food was prepared from the plentiful stores, and people got to work.

Hendricks, Geiger, Stevens, and Amir ate and prepared themselves. Annie had worked the previous evening instructing others how to increase the battery life of two drones by fixing extra power cells to the point where the added weight did not detract from the additional power supplied. Using the lighter weight batteries from the radios helped negate some of that, but even those modifications added minutes instead of hours. Annie said that she would counter that by 'parking' the drones whenever she could, by nestling them on tree tops to save the energy required to keep them in a hover. She planned to leapfrog the flying devices in order to allow a relay of information and keep herself in command of the data feed, and she could cover the distance with three drones, which still left one patrolling the enclave and one in reserve. Her calculations didn't need to be checked, because a human would only waste an hour doing the math just to find that the super-computer was right the first time.

Without ceremony the four-man team slipped out of the gates, which closed behind them, and headed north.

By the time lunch was announced, my nerve was beginning to break. I'd asked Annie a dozen times how they were doing, but each time she gave me an annoyingly vague progress report along the lines of them still being on course, or that they were moving as expected.

It wasn't until the late afternoon that she quietly told me they had found the town, or whatever it was.

"Check your tablet," she told me.

Without fuss, I took myself away to a quiet corner and checked that nobody was watching me before I swiped the little tough tablet into life and watched as a screen ballooned to fill the display and show me what looked like action-camera footage. The screen flashed the headphone icon at me, and I reeled out the attached earbuds and put them in. The footage came to life as the sounds of rustling clothing and breathing accompanied the images.

It was from Amir's camera, the small high definition unit attached to the radio worn on the chest of his equipment vest. His viewpoint encompassed the backs of Geiger and Stevens, both on one knee and scanning wide arcs of fire in unison. Directly in front of Amir was Hendricks, who was carefully removing his weapons. Placing his short-barreled assault rifle gently against a waxy tree trunk, he removed the four spare magazines from his vest, unfastening the whole section, then unclipped the drop-leg holster from his belt and removed the whole thing before adding his spare ammunition for that too. His hands reached forward, and I heard the sound of more ripping Velcro as he removed the holster, sidearm, and spare magazines from Amir's vest. His hand went to the knife sheathed on his vest, but he paused, obviously deciding whether to go in totally unarmed and deciding that a knife wouldn't be seen as a technological advantage.

He looked intently forward, just above and to the left of the camera, obviously at where Amir's face was.

"You ready for this?" he said, making the eye contact matter as he fixed him with a stare.

"I'm okay," Amir muttered back, making Hendricks shake him and ask again.

"I'm ready," Amir said back in a louder voice, evidently convincing Hendricks that he was.

"Okay, let's go then," he said, turning his eyes away and rising up out of sight of the camera. Amir took a few steadying breaths, then rose to follow, leaving me with a glimpse of Stevens offering a nod toward him. I fought down the urge to nod back, such was the emotion contained in the simple gesture. I swallowed down the feelings which were assaulting me: fear, guilt for watching them, nervous tension. Ten minutes of close-up footage showing a mixture of Hendricks' back and dense foliage followed, which I watched intently as though taking my eyes off the screen would somehow curse them.

"Dr. Anderson?" came a raised female voice from behind me, making me jump pulling the earbuds out and let out a small, strangled cry as I tried to hide the tablet from her sight. I turned to see the tall medical doctor, who I knew was called Kelly, but we had never really spoken much.

"Sorry," I said, "I was, er …"

"No need to explain," she said, holding up a hand and wearing a tight smile of embarrassment, "we all need our releases. Anyway, I was hoping to speak to you regarding the computer control of some of our medical equipment?"

"Yes, er, I …" I stammered, "but you could just ask Annie and she could tell you if she can manage it or not."

"Oh," she said, pulling a face which clearly indicated how taken aback she was.

"Annie?" I asked, still looking slightly up out of habit. She responded via the nearest speaker, which was part of a computer terminal, with a loud chime of acknowledgment.

"How can I help, Dr. Warren?" she said in a sweet, businesslike tone.

"I was wondering," she said hesitantly, her head inclined up but her eyes watching me warily, "if you could assist with the control of some of our medical equipment?"

"I'm happy to assess your needs and offer solutions. Shall we discuss this further in the medical area?"

"Yes, er …" She shot me a final glance for help, but I just smiled. "I'll, er, meet you there?"

"That's fine, Dr. Warren."

As I watched her walk away, her words finally dawned on me, making me shout after her.

"I wasn't," I yelled, stopping myself just in time, "it was research footage Annie was showing me," I finished lamely, seeing her turn back and offer me an embarrassed smile.

Sitting down again, defeated, I looked back to the tablet and put the earbuds back in to drown out the mocking laughter from Annie on the speaker.

Unaware that they were being monitored, at least by anyone except Annie who they saw as their technical backup, Amir and Hendricks stepped out of the dense jungle and into a clearing which spread out before them until the high, wooden and metal walls rose at a right angle to the flat ground to loom upwards.

Those walls, Hendricks noted, were a good deal higher than their own metal ring of space pods. Shouts ahead of them rang out, and noises from inside the walls drifted down to them.

"Hold your arms out," Hendricks muttered to Amir, who copied the gesture and spread his arms to show an unthreatening pose and to prove that he carried no weapons. Keeping their hands spread wide, both men continued side by side toward the gate until a shouted challenge halted them twenty paces away.

"Stop there!" called a harsh, guttural voice from above the gate.

Both men stopped, waiting for the next instruction. They had discussed their plan on the long journey there, deciding to withhold the fact that they had met Harrison and Tori from Three Hills, or that they knew a version of events which placed these people in the category of being the bad guys, and decided to announce their presence simply to their neighbors.

"Who are you?" came the next shout, prompting Hendricks to clear his throat.

"We came down from space," he shouted back, "didn't you see us?"

A face appeared above the wooden ramparts, presumably belonging to the man who shouted at them, and he regarded them quizzically. He turned back, clearly conversing with someone else, then turned back to shout.

"What do you want?" he yelled finally.

"We want to talk to"—he paused, almost mentioning Tanaka's name and cursing himself silently—"whoever is in charge here."

No answer came for a while, making the two men stood in front of the gates increasingly nervous, until the heavy gates creaked open.

The scene before them widened to show a man stood centrally, wearing a battered jacket of dark brown leather. His arms were behind his back, and his face showed a look of hard-bitten malevolence. He did not, in any way, seem like a man capable of kindness.

He was flanked on both sides by larger men holding an array of weapons ranging from bows to spears, all of which were held low toward the strangers. All of those weapons then turned to bow to their leader, with a worn semi-automatic handgun holstered at the front of the leather jacket man's waist.

"I am in charge here," he announced in a voice far deeper than he should possess. "I am The Tanaka, and we had almost given up hope of you coming back down to the surface. Please, come in. Welcome to the Hot Springs.

Chapter 27

AN OUTBREAK OF DEMOCRACY

Harrison and Tori kept up a hard pace back to Three Hills. Although still relatively safe to be outside of their walls during darkness, a side effect of living their lives as they did was an almost genetically coded fear of the dark. A fear of the dark when not inside a walled compound, that is.

In truth, very few of his people felt these worries. Very few of them had ever seen The Swarm, but most had heard the chirping, screeching noise it made as it washed around their town walls most months.

In the time that Harrison had taken control, he had brought a new feeling to the town and people were generally happier. He met regularly with people who built, who farmed both animals and crops, and those who made things inside the walls, and he spoke on behalf of the warriors and the defenders. He asked for each section of the town, as made up of each subsequent extension, to appoint a spokesperson to meet with him and others, and that it was up to each part of the town to decide how they chose their representative. He met regularly with the group of ten representatives and heard the words they brought from the people.

Ultimately, he had the final say in everything, but his new ideas ushered in a time of transparency. He listened to the concerns of his people, and even if he didn't always act on those concerns, at least most knew that he could be petitioned on their behalf.

In the last three years, since his rise, he had listened to the pleas of his people about their overcrowding and had organized massive work parties into the jungles where the nearest big swathes of tall trees were felled, and their trunks split to build new segments outside the existing wall, which had stood from before anyone still alive had been there. These extensions to the town had allowed for more space so that people weren't living in overcrowded conditions in too-close proximity to the precious animals which were kept inside the walls to prevent the meat from being flensed from their bones in the night. The original walls still stood, as there was no good sense in taking them down, and the new walls bulged outwards with new gates being cut into the ancient timbers allowing access to the central part of the settlement.

The work had taken up every daylight hour, brought people together, and raised the spirits of the town as a whole. He had allowed parties to visit the sea. He had encouraged their young ones to be educated to a good standard and raised the age at which they had to work. In short, people were happy under his rule. He had kept them safe from Tanaka's people at the Springs, and they were confident that he would be capable of defending them.

When the bright lights burned in the skies, and the billowing white clouds dropped gently to the earth in the near distance, Harrison had known that the legends were true. They had all grown up hearing the stories, about how there were others like their first settlers who had fled the planet to space instead of going underground, but most believed the stories to be a tale for children; some symbolic hope that others survived, and that it wasn't just them who had remained of their race which had once covered the earth on all continents.

Harrison had all but dismissed the legends, as dreaming about a past he couldn't be sure even existed offered him no help in the present, but when he saw the first pods falling he knew it was real. He knew, and he believed with a burning intensity he had never felt before, that the arrival of their space-going brethren could mean an end to the violence between the two biggest groups of survivors, and maybe even an end to The Swarm.

Now, breathing hard and matching pace with his lighter companion who sprang gracefully through the dense trees just ahead of him, two thoughts struck him simultaneously.

Firstly, he was certain that he had done the right thing by talking to the newcomers and being totally honest about their situation. He believed that they would help him, even if they didn't outright agree to join his fight against a man and his followers who, he believed, actually preferred hostilities to safety.

The second thing he thought of, was that as soon as he was back, he would wash and change then get Tori back to his room. They would need to eat at some point, but that ranked lower in his personal priorities.

Arriving back in the proximity of the town, approaching from the flat, southerly direction, Harrison called out with a noise like the cry of a large bird. On his third cry, he heard it returned in a deeper, distant sounding voice. His sentries knew he was coming, and he knew they were expecting him.

He felt secure in that knowledge; it meant he was less likely to fetch an arrow or three fired from atop the walls.

Breaking through the tree line and into the clearing, where the felled trees had given the ground away to hard-packed dust, they slowed to a walk as they crossed the remaining fifty meters to the gateway. Harrison sniffed the air and looked up to the sky, then glanced to Tori who just nodded her agreement to his unspoken thought. Already people were bringing livestock back inside after their day spent in the pens to feed, and the flow of people returning from their crop fields was steady and kept the gates open, just as the first fat, heavy rain drops of the sudden shower began to fall.

Accepting waves and pats on their shoulders as they returned, Harrison felt a wave of happiness and gratitude wash over him; he genuinely loved his people, even if he didn't know most of them, and he knew he would do everything he could to make their lives better. There were over a thousand people in their town, and all of them looking ultimately to him for their protection was not a burden he shied away from. Nor did he take it lightly.

He was bombarded with questions, and he knew that the second thought he had when running back was, sadly, going to have to wait. As was the shower he was anticipating, but it seemed that the rainfall would have to suffice. As the crowd of people asking questions of him began to thicken, he stopped trying to force his way through and held up his hands for quiet.

He told them that he had spoken to the people from space, and that they were friendly. He told them that he wanted to assemble the town representatives immediately, which appeased the masses and let him carry on his way. In the press, he had lost Tori who had used the distraction he had caused by speaking to slip away, and she had made it to his room first where he found her already using the shower.

Deciding that the representatives would have to wait, he smiled as he knew the second thought on his mind was back on the table.

An hour later and combining the meeting with food and drink to save on time and discomfort, he apologized to the representatives for both his delay and for eating as they spoke but reminded them that he had covered a great distance in a short time. They allowed him both liberties unquestioningly, mostly as everyone there wanted to know the details.

He gave those details, often allowing Tori to take over and give the descriptions from her point of view which invariably added perceptions which he had missed. He wasn't conscious of it, but this was one of the main reasons he was such a respected and effective leader at a young age; he listened to his people. He interjected when Tori began to give enthusiastic specifics about the weapons they carried, about the new guns which would give them the edge in a fight against Tanaka, and he deftly steered the subject away from conflict as he had not informed the others of their foray to The Source. Knowing that he had no chance to delay this and hoping that the news would be clouded by the arrival of the others, he told the brief and mostly bloodless story about their skirmish bluntly.

He finished by reassuring them that The Keepers were taken by surprise and that they had removed the bodies, so even when Tanaka found their people missing, he would not be able to directly accuse them.

"As for the others," he said through a mouthful of tasty, greasy meat wrapped in a freshly cooked flatbread, "we will visit them again after the high moon."

All in all, after an action-packed few days, Harrison was pleased with himself and hopeful for the future. Anticipating some rest as they sealed up their gates tightly for the brightest nights, he had no idea of the events he had set into motion.

Hendricks' camera now showed on the left side of my screen as Amir's showed opposite it. The earbuds were back, only this time in just my left ear, so I wouldn't get caught out by anyone approaching again and act like a kid caught using an internet site that wanted a credit card number. Still, when Cat called my name from the door-way of the small shelter I had commandeered for my projects, of which I really had none but needed an excuse to be on my own for at least some time every day, I still jumped like I'd been caught with porn again.

"God*dammit*," I cursed, hearing her light laugh tickle the air like the high notes on a piano, "why does everyone enjoy sneaking up on me?" I said, albeit with a half-smile as I turned to her.

"Maybe you could program, sorry, *ask*, Annie to give you a proximity warning? Or maybe I should wear a bell?" she said with a smile that could unlock a bank vault.

"I'm sorry," she said as she cleared her throat and put on an attempted serious face and failing marginally. "Are you hungry or shall I come back when you've finished doing … whatever it is you're doing?"

"I'm not," I said almost angrily, "I mean I wasn't … why does everyone assume that?"

"It's fine," she said, laughing again, "I brought all ten seasons of Game of Thrones on my tablet, but each to their own I guess?"

Leaning back and clapping both hands to my face I let out a defeated groan. As I did so, the tablet lay on my lap and gave her a look at the screen.

"Is that Mr. Hendricks?" she asked, all joviality vanished in an instant.

Sitting back up and snatching at the tablet, I realized it was too late to pretend that it was anything else. Regarding her slightly worried expression and the covered plate in her hand, I decided I best let her in on at least some of what was going on.

"Is that for me?" I asked, pointing at the plate and seeing her nod in answer. "Then you better sit down, and I'll tell you."

The one remaining earbud in my left ear made a noise. It was a noise of a woman clearing her throat, and I knew exactly what it meant.

"Annie?" I said aloud, hearing an angry chime report back from the tablet speakers, even though I had the earbud activated. The chime was full of bass, like the computer program had her hands on her hips as she glared at me. "I need to bring Catarina up to speed on a few things, that alright with you?"

Another double down-tone came, full of resignation. I think I read that one right as Annie saying that my idea was 'fine.' Or that I could 'do whatever I want.'

Maybe it was even a 'wow.'

I got the impression she would roast me later. Obviously some of the dialogue interaction discretion protocols and subroutines were still my original coding, but I was sure she'd get around to rewriting those eventually.

Cat sat next to me and handed me the plate, which I put to the side straight away and looked at her.

"What I'm going to tell you *has* to stay between us, okay?" She hesitated but nodded anyway.

"Hendricks and Amir are talking to the other big group which have settled here, the ones who didn't come here to find us. Annie has a live link to their radios and cameras which she's relaying back through the radios of Stevens and Geiger who are hidden near their town, and then through three drones which she's parked up high on treetops to relay back to her here. With me so far?" I asked. She gave me a blank look and a slight head tilt which clearly said, *duh*, so I carried on.

"Great, they've met the main guy and have had a tour of the town which up until now has mostly been showing off how many people they have with weapons I think; it's like they've got everyone out on parade for their benefit."

"But what are they saying?" she asked, making me remove the earbud and retract them back into the tablet casing so that the speaker came back to life. I turned it up a couple of notches, then back down as I didn't want the sound carrying outside.

We both listened, huddled in close to the screen in silence, as the main guy showed on both halves of the screen.

Chapter 28

THE ART OF TELLING LIES

Tanaka wasn't a big man, but his eyes spoke to Hendricks of such a capability for cruelty that he had almost made up his mind within minutes of meeting him.

They had been led grandly, although the word 'paraded' came to mind, through the streets and to what appeared to be the main hall. Inside, women with revealing outfits adorned the big chair assumed to be a throne in some parody of sci-fi films of sixty years ago.

Nine hundred and eighty years ago, Hendricks reminded himself.

The display was almost childlike in a way, as though they were being shown all of their new acquaintance's new toys, but the barely disguised underlying air of malevolence was difficult to ignore. They were given drinks, offered small samples of food which they assumed was a delicacy, and invited to sit. As soon as they did, three young women sat close behind them and stroked their gentle hands over the shoulders of the visitors, no doubt in an attempt to distract and disarm them, but it had the opposite effect and made both of them feel distinctly uneasy.

"So," began Tanaka as two other women snaked themselves around his small shoulders, "you are from the time of the first settlers?"

Hendricks and Amir exchanged a look, the echo of Hendricks' briefing flickering between their eyes.

"Yes," Amir answered, mindful not to boast that, if anything, he was the original 'first settler,' or at least he was supposed to be because the whole thing had been his idea, his design, and ultimately his money which was directly responsible for every living person he saw there. They had agreed, or at least Amir had agreed to Hendricks' suggestion, that they should keep the talking to a minimum.

"Tell me," Tanaka said as he leaned back and allowed the snaking hands to roll across his small chest, "is it cold up above the clouds?"

Hendricks took the reins to answer, leaning forward away from the girl caressing his back. "We wouldn't know. We assume so, but we were all asleep and we have no idea why we were up there so long. We were asleep before we went up, and we woke up back on Earth."

Tanaka smiled, as though the person he was interrogating had given his story and now sat resolute and tight-lipped, unwilling to give up any more. He knew how to give those people incentive to speak.

"You must stay here, as our guests," he said grandly, changing the subject.

"We would be honored," Amir answered with the slightest bow of his head and a flat hand held on his chest, "but our people are waiting for us back at our camp."

"I insist," Tanaka responded, leaning forward just enough to change the atmosphere of the small group and making two of the girls shy away slightly.

"We really can't, I am very sorry," Hendricks cut in wearing a disarming smile. "Perhaps another time?"

Tanaka's face changed from one of menace to one of resigned humor; both expressions, Hendricks believed, were utterly false.

"Another time," he conceded, "I was hoping you could witness one of our most treasured rituals, one that has been passed down for hundreds of years among our people, but this can only happen at night unfortunately …"

Amir glanced to Hendricks, meaning to exchange another look, but the Brit pointedly refused to acknowledge his eye contact. For their eyes to meet, and for the knowing look to be given and received, would betray to Tanaka that these naive settlers from space knew what happened during the nights in this new hell they had landed in.

"Can we return in a few weeks, when we have settled in?" Amir asked, falling back to their rehearsed script which they had practiced on their humid and physically taxing journey there.

"Settlers from space are always welcome at the Springs," Tanaka said magnanimously with a wide spread of his small hands, which pulled the waist of his leather jacket open enough to show the worn grip of the gun he wore in the belt holster. "But perhaps we will come to visit your home next time?"

Hendricks successfully hid his true feelings behind a face which displayed a smile of gratitude, with a hint of excitement at further meetings. Amir, for all his years of dominating boardrooms and courtrooms, failed miserably. Of all the meetings he had been in where he had issued threats in many guises or simply laid out the full truth of everything he and his company could do, of all the times he had negotiated with people who were key to his plans but had never known the full extent of their personal worth, he squandered all of that experience, and he failed.

In hindsight, much later, he knew he had folded under the pressure. This was the first time in his life that the stakes were high enough that he could actually lose. It had always been wealth, or reputation, or power in the past, and all of those things were easily replaced with a glib statement to the press and an ambiguous offer of an exciting new project. Never, not even in the poker dens in Calcutta or in the underground gambling pits of Hong Kong and Thailand, had he ever truly been in physical danger. Even when in the worst peril for a rich man in third-world countries and at risk of a high-level kidnapping he had never been in any real peril, because the men he employed had always been there to shield him from the threat.

Men like Tanaka, the original one at least, had always put their own bodies between him and the risks he courted.

Now, unsupported by a global network of contacts and billions of dollars at his disposal, he faced the danger and he completely blew it.

The face he pulled, only momentarily, and the look of panic he threw in desperation to the quietly polite man beside him who was pretending not to be a killer hiding beneath his mask, told Tanaka everything he needed to know.

He knew that these men were afraid of him. He knew that they knew what happened in the night during the full moon, and he knew that they were afraid of Tanaka's warriors paying them a visit. On top of what he knew, there were also things he suspected.

He suspected that Harrison and the fools from the Hills had beaten him to the prize of meeting the newcomers. He suspected that, given their equipment and the fact that only one of them carried a single knife, that they possessed weapons which he could use to turn the tide in his favor for another hundred years. That suspected knowledge made his analytical brain search for a way that could be done safely, and he formed the assumption that there were others waiting away from the camp.

He doubted, even with their superior technology and weapons, that the few people who had so recently come from their long sleep in space, were quite ready to face his whole army. He couldn't risk using The Swarm against them, because he wanted their people alive to show him how their equipment worked, so he decided that he would turn his attention to them.

As soon as he had dealt with the deserter and dealt a crippling blow to the Hills in retaliation for attacking The Keepers of The Source.

Hendricks, a master of many skills and not all of them physical or tactical, was a man well versed in the subtle psychological warfare of an interview. He recognized the face that Amir Weatherby made, and he knew that the man who had dreams of becoming the great leader he wanted to be had failed them all.

Miles to the south, both in unhappy silence, Anderson and Catarina watched the jerky movements on screen as Hendricks and Amir were shown the exit in the high wooden walls and began their journey into the jungle where they met with Geiger and Stevens and relayed the story.

The one line which stung the minds of the two people watching through the cameras on their chests came from Hendricks before the screen went black.

"Whatever he says, that man wants to rule everything… and we have just stepped right in the middle of this war whether we like it or not."

Exchanging their own looks which made no attempt to hide their fear, the speaker crackled gently in to life. Annie actually cleared her throat, a development which Anderson completely missed partly because it was so human and natural, before she gave her own report and opinion.

"They have met up with the others now. They should be back by dark, which isn't ideal."

"You're telling me," Anderson replied before an idea hit him through fear for his friends. "Can you keep the drones up all the way back for them?"

"Yes," she replied, "battery levels should hold; I won't bore you with the specifics."

Chapter 29

THE SWARM

Hendricks and his team made it back just as the last light faded rapidly over the horizon, much to the relief of everyone including the four sweat-soaked men who relaxed visibly as soon as they were safely inside the protection of the walls.

As the gates clicked loudly together with the lock engaging audibly, the air of being granted a reprieve washed over the weary men. They tried to reassure themselves that there was no reason for The Swarm to suddenly become active a day before they were due to stalk the shadows cast by the full moon.

Still, experiencing the stress that was induced by the fear of sharing the earth with the terrifyingly destructive force that was made more frightening by their lack of knowledge surrounding them, was not an enjoyable experience.

The four ate, washed, and rested, and over breakfast the following day gave their report of what happened at the Springs. Everyone who was present had seen the footage by then, and when Hendricks gave his commentary alongside the replay it gave the others more insight into the things that even high-definition camera footage couldn't capture.

"In short," Hendricks finished in his precise tones, "I believe that Harrison has given us the more accurate version of events on the surface, and I sense nothing but hostile intentions from Tanaka's people. The very fact that they wanted us to stay for the full moon at their town was cause enough for concern."

"So," Nathalie asked from her seat in the corner, "we need to choose sides?"

"Yes," Amir said, butting in to answer the question asked of Hendricks. "It's like when two companies are fighting to acquire a rival," he began, narcissistically likening the situation to a subject in which he would be the sole expert in the room, "and they have different tactics. One will offer support and an opportunity to grow, the other will invoke fear and use their own panic to drive down the price."

He looked around the room to see if they were following him. They were not.

"Imagine this," he went on, digging a deeper hole, "if a rival company of one of mine were trying to acquire or merge with the third-largest company in that field, then they would own a sufficient portion of the market to be able to drive down prices and force my company to react or become less profitable. I would obviously want to prevent that, so I would approach that other company with a better offer and a different approach to ensure that I instead of them cornered the market …"

Realizing too late that he had totally lost the room, he turned to Hendricks for support.

"It's a simple matter of what kind of people we want to be," he said. "Our moral compasses should point toward Harrison's group because they are the closest thing to a democracy here we have seen, whereas Tanaka is basically a warlord. That's my recommendation."

It was a recommendation that was supported readily by everyone, even Amir who had been trying to make the same point but using a now extinct reference base which only he seemed to understand.

"Other items," Annie said to the meeting, as though she were working from an agenda that only she had seen, "The Swarm is due to be active any time from tonight for the next five days but given anecdotal evidence from Harrison it is likely that they will only be active for the three days surrounding the full moon. I have analyzed the patterns and tried to re-establish satellite camera control without success, and the previous still-frame footage is still being reviewed."

"So," Anderson asked, "you're saying that The Swarm might or might not come any time for the next five days, but nobody can be certain?"

"Reminds me of the criminal profiler they brought in for that Belgium job," Hendricks said as he turned to Magda, the woman who had worked on the Interpol surveillance team with him. She laughed in response, a loud bark of humor that ripped from her mouth and broke her characteristic silence. Even Annie stayed silent, waiting for the private joke to be shared. Hendricks, seeing the expectant faces watching them, told the story.

"We were after a serial killer, but he was on the Interpol radar because it was a fanatical motivation and classed as terrorism. That and the fact that he'd left four bodies in three countries by the time we were called in. Anyway, we had a gag order on the European news community so the profiler they'd sent in only had the case files to work from …" He trailed off as the memory tickled him into light laughter again.

Magda leaned forward and picked up the story, resting her elbows on her knees in a feminine yet very male-orientated pose.

"He was from your American FBI," she said with a smirk, "and it went …" She paused as she controlled another outbreak of laughter which threatened to stop their story entirely.

"It went like this," Anderson said, taking over and putting on a very exaggerated accent as he raised one eyebrow theatrically, "you're lookin' for a killer who is driven and calculating, but might also be random in the way they choose their victims. He, or maybe she, is either black or white unless they are from an Arab country, and they are violent. *Very* violent. They pro—" He paused to cough and fix his face to be able to continue. "They probably had an abusive childhood, or they could have been completely normal …" Magda burst out laughing again, having been barely able to keep it inside as Hendricks spoke, and now forced him to devolve into hysterics with her. Their laughter had been infectious and, although none of them fully appreciated the story as they weren't there, the others also laughed.

"So, you're implying that I'm giving you a bland profile of nonsense?" Annie asked in a careful tone, forcing Hendricks to contain himself and answer with equal caution.

"Not at all," he said apologetically, "it just reminded me of that guy. He went all over the world trotting out that bullshit and I think we were the first people to call him on it."

"Well the assessment still stands," she said snappily, "and if nobody else has anything pressing, we should resume our duties."

Filing out as though we had been told off, we melted away to our duties. Elliot and I had been finalizing the rigging-up of another cryotube for use as a bug catcher using the identical setup as the other one, which we had found almost full of water from the downpours of tropical rain. Working with a seemingly terse Annie, we tested it to ensure it worked fine before retreating back inside. The evening meal in the main tent seemed to swell to an evening recreation period as nobody melted away in ones and twos to their own corners of the compound like normal.

Maybe it was the feeling that The Swarm would come and wash around us that night, which for most would be their first experience of the awful screeching noise they brought with them, and perhaps people wanted to be closest to the guns.

As a contingency, Annie had prepared a dozen pods to be used as lifeboats, and people would scramble into them and seal the hatches. She was pretty sure that not even the big bugs could chew through the space-grade titanium alloy.

Whatever it was, the main shelter buzzed with the sound of so many people all talking together, and it reminded me a little of parties back in the old days. Turning and seeing the tall blonde woman I had embarrassed myself in front of the day before, I raised my voice over the din to try and be heard.

"Dr. Warren," I said loudly with a smile, "about yesterday," I began, hoping that my face offered the sense that I was apologizing, just not apologizing for the thing that she thought I should be apologizing for.

"Dr. Anderson," she said, a hint of resignation in her reply, "no need to explain, Annie has informed me that you weren't … that you were watching something else."

"Oh," I said, "that's good then …" and trailed off, waiting for the subject change to come from her. It didn't, and I felt suddenly as though I had overstayed my welcome standing near her. Just as I was about to deliver an "Okay then," and sidle away, she turned to me and gripped my forearm.

"Can you tell me why my entire medical team is on standby?" she blurted out.

I was shocked. *Did people really not know the full extent of the things happening here?*

"I assume it's because of the heightened risk from the bugs being active around a full moon?" I tried, not sure if I was right to tell her. Her eyes dropped, as though she were crestfallen by the affirmation of what she feared. I spoke again and clumsily tried to change the subject.

"Listen, do you want to get a drink and maybe talk somewhere?"

"I was hoping it wasn't that," she said, then walked away without another word, leaving me openmouthed in the middle of the room. Before I could gather myself, my elbow was gripped from behind and I was walked toward the exit. A slim hand of soft tanned skin reached out to press the door release button and I walked out into the thick, humid air of the night which had chilled rapidly.

"In terms you can hopefully understand … If you're hoping to code that particular subroutine," said the rich accent from behind my shoulder as I turned, "you should probably realize by now that she needs a female to female hardline connector …"

I stared down at Cat, trying to figure out what she meant. My eyebrows disconnected above my nose as my eyes went wide with the sudden understanding of what she had said. I had no answer, literally nothing to say, so the silence stretched out as her smile grew wider in fractions until she finally let out a laugh at my discomfort.

"I had no idea ..." I said, feeling foolish.

"She's not your type, anyway," Cat said with comedy dismissiveness.

"Oh," I answered, "and what is my type?"

She seemed to hesitate, showing a crinkle in her smooth brow in the low light coming from bulb above the shelter entrance. "I would have hoped your type was smaller and darker," she said hopefully as she stepped closer and looked up toward my face.

Mesmerized by the moment, everything else forgotten, Annie chose the best time to interrupt proceedings. My flash on annoyance was destroyed, however, and replaced instantly with sudden, urgent, and gut-churning fear.

"Movement, three hundred meters, large body approaching."

~

The screams of the woman, now stripped and beaten just enough to force her compliance into the thick ropes which bound her wrists and ankles, echoed loudly throughout the jungle and bounced back irregularly. Her screams might attract The Swarm, or they might not, but either way Tanaka would be amazed if she survived the night.

He had done this once before, with a servant who had stolen food from him if he recalled correctly, and although The Swarm had not come the servant was nonetheless found dead the following morning without a mark on them. His people had claimed that their soul had fled the body in cowardice, leaving behind the empty meat and bone.

This night though, he fancied that he could already hear the shrieking, deafening chirping noise that they made when they came toward them.

Waiting less than an hour, during which time the screams had faded into only sporadic bursts of wailing sound, The Swarm found their offering and rolled over the body of the woman like a living, crawling blanket. Her screams, much renewed by the arrival of the bugs, were drowned out with such suddenness that the change in pitch from hysterical fear to agonizing pain was almost imperceptible. The pulsating, roiling mass of shapes each occasionally flashing an oily reflection from their armored bodies, rolled over the woman in minutes until her flesh had been consumed and only the disorganized bones were left among a patch of darker earth. The Swarm moved onwards, leaving nothing behind and moving past the high walls of the Springs as though they were programmed to ignore them.

"Yes," Tanaka said with evil relish, "keep going that way," as he raised his eyes to the darkness, in the distant direction of Three Hills.

~

"Drones are up," Annie snapped into our radios, "all non-essential personnel have been instructed to stay inside."

Hendricks, along with his entire team, converged on the central three pods as planned. Others joined us there, me arriving first as I had already been outside, and we waited for the report from the aerial footage, as much as that could tell us.

"Okay," Annie said, "two large groups converging from the same direction, one hundred meters apart, two hundred meters out. Painting them now."

With that, two drones surged toward the incoming swarms and deployed a payload of IR-visible paint which cascaded over the individual bugs and gave a better sight picture through the goggles and the optics of the drones.

"Automated gun systems are operational, on standby," Annie added.

We waited, everyone breathing at differing rates and making the tension in the air thicker than the humidity.

"They've reached the walls," Annie said before pausing, "staying at ground level, moving around the perimeter ... approaching the cryotraps, standby ..."

We waited, most of us holding our breath if the sudden change in sound was anything to go by.

"Traps closed," Annie announced, "five subjects contained, sedating them ..." We all relaxed slightly, realizing that we had been worrying over something that had actually turned out to be pretty simple after all. Simple, that is, until Annie spoke again.

"No response to anesthesia. Increasing levels, still no response, increasing again ..."

We all exchanged looks of horror on hearing the terseness in her voice, until she finally let us off the hook.

"Subjects subdued, decreasing temperature. Recommend one subject restrained in a controlled environment and others kept on ice," she finished, satisfaction and a hint of relief in her tone.

Elliot nodded to me which made me automatically respond to the gesture without knowing what I was letting myself in for.

"We can do that with the biology guys," he offered on my behalf, but I was too weak to risk appearing weak and backing out. Elliot made to start toward the gates when Annie spoke directly to him through his earpiece. Nobody else responded, but I was let in on the private conversation. "Dr. Whitmore," she said in a smooth, hushed voice, "might I recommend that you wait until daylight so as not to go outside the gates when there are swarms of dangerous creatures outside?"

"Good idea," I heard him mutter, as he turned to style out his initial movement and pretend he wasn't planning on opening the front door after all.

Retreating inside for a restless night, I waited for the next morning's excitement.

⁓

That excitement was less enjoyable than any of them would have thought, when Annie quietly informed them that they should only open the pods in a secure environment with significant armed support. A sobering thought for before breakfast, but a task that should be completed before the majority of their population was active.

A select few, annoyingly for him Anderson was chosen to be one of them, sealed themselves inside a small shelter and activated the internal lights. Weber had selected a large shotgun of a bullpup design and was mindful to keep the gaping maw of the business end pointed directly at the glass as it hissed and popped open.

Wearing thick gloves and reaching in carefully, one of the scientists picked up a frosted thing, curled up and looking a little like a woodlouse on the back, with a shining head and big mandibles. He made a noise like he was going to sneeze at any point as he moved the inanimate bug, and wore a facial expression of pure, sickened horror. The glass lid hissed back down, no doubt controlled by Annie, and the frozen bug was placed down onto a solid plastic board where heavy straps were ratcheted around its body.

The first thing to hit them, was the sheer size of it. They were all accustomed to the fact that, in their minds at least, bugs only grew to about the size of a human hand at the biggest.

These things, seeming more alien than insect, were the size of small cats. The head and jaws were like big biting ants, but the midsection and fat tail end were armored like a big beetle.

All sorts of noises of awe and disgust came from the people present, right up until the thing gave a violent spasm to strain against the straps with its wide, snapping jaws clapping together like a jackhammer. As one, everybody in the room screamed and jumped back, all except Dieter Weber who calmly squeezed the trigger of his shotgun and obliterated the creature instantly as the heavy shot tore through its carapace and ripped into the thin sheet wall of the shelter behind. As the sound echoed and people's hearing returned to normal, their biologist shot Weber a disgusted look of annoyance and hit the release button to open the glass of the cryopod again. The lid rose, stopped, then closed again, prompting confusion as the release was hit again. It didn't move, and Annie's voice filled their ears.

"Wait," she snapped, "before Dieter shot it, the bug emitted a signal."

"A what?" Anderson asked incredulously.

"A signal," she answered, "it sent out a wireless request for command code. It couldn't … I think it couldn't detect a network so it just … reacted … David, I'm putting it on your screen."

"Hold on a second," Hendricks said as he looked slightly upwards to a speaker that wasn't there, "you're saying this thing is remote controlled?"

"No, not remote controlled, it's part of a network," Anderson said quietly as he tapped at the keyboard, "a bio-command network, like an ant hive."

"So that's normal then?" Hendricks asked. He would have sworn at that moment, that if they could, Dr. David Anderson and Annie would have exchanged a knowing look.

"That would be normal, yes," Anderson answered, spinning around the screen to show him lines of symbols and numbers that he didn't understand.

"But?" he asked the computer programmer.

"But they're using *MY* code to do it," Annie answered, for the first time displaying a genuine hint of fear in her voice.

Chapter 30

THE NEEDS OF THE MANY

Feeling rested and safe, Harrison patrolled the ramparts of the high walls in front of his town. The guards, all volunteers, who would keep watch over their people during the brightest of the dark nights greeted him with admiration and respect. The rumors of the newcomers from space, with their superior technology and their total lack of understanding of their new home, had spread like a fire in dry grass. The people believed in Harrison, believed in his ability to lead them safely into a new era where at least one threat could be dealt with, and they could live in happier and more peaceful times.

He always did this, and even took regular night duties on the wall himself to protect his people from harm, but tonight he had taken the night off after his recent exertions, and made his rounds as the sun was setting because Tori had told him she wanted him back in their bed as soon as possible. He was eager to abide by her command, but he was sure to abide by his own standards before he went to her.

If anything, the act of being out on the walls at a dangerous time only served to heighten his anticipation.

Walking every part of their defenses and setting foot on each fire step to exchange words with his people, he stopped to congratulate a young man on the birth of his first child and asked him if he would not rather be at home with the baby and his woman. Standing tall with a shock of almost white-blonde hair, his answer that he would get more sleep on the walls than at home made the men and women around him laugh raucously, as he knew the answer would, and Harrison smiled at him as he walked away, reminding himself to reward the man and his woman for having a healthy child.

Finding his way back to his room, he peeled off his stiff leather vest with his long knives still strapped to the back of it and smiled down to Tori.

In the dead of the night, Harrison woke up and sat bolt upright. The sound which had ripped him from a satisfied, deep sleep was undeniably a scream. A scream here, so far from the walls, terrified him.

Flying from the bed he threw on his pants and boots, stooping to snatch up his vest and blades as he blasted from the room to head toward the ramparts at a sprint.

When he hit the walls, ignoring the shouts and questions coming from those he passed, another sensation assaulted him. It hit his nose and his eyes, and he knew what it was long before he found the place in the newest section of wall that was ablaze. The closer he got to it, the more people he saw fleeing inwards toward the gate into the old part of the town.

As he found the section ablaze, yet another sensation struck him. Above the sounds of the crackling fire and the shouts and screams coming from the people, came the high-pitched whining screech of The Swarm.

Looking down and squinting his eyes against the acrid smoke coming from the burning timbers at the base of the wall, the screeching noise rose in intensity as a single chunk of burning wood fell inwards to land with an ominous and resounding thud against the packed earth below.

That sound and the horrifying vision that accompanied it, was rapidly followed by the inexorable flow of dark, shining shapes pouring through the gap to be illuminated by the flames. Their black carapaces reflected the light of the fire, highlighting them as they burst through the wall to spread out in search of flesh to consume.

Harrison, frozen momentarily in dreadful dismay, watched the shining black flood disappear between the huts below just as new screams wafted up to him; screams, this time, of the animals left trapped to their fate as their masters fled toward safety.

Sparked into action, Harrison's feet started to move his body fast back toward the gate where the old town met the new even before he consciously knew he was doing it. He looked down to the gate which was thronged with a mass of people panicking and pushing their way through the gap as they desperately sought safety from the terror pouring in behind them.

From his unique vantage point, Harrison could see the whole scene spread out below him in almost slow-motion. The gap in the outer wall behind him still admitted a steady stream of reflective black bodies highlighted by the flames, and beneath him a crowd of men and women, some carrying animals and children, were all trying to pack though a gateway that wasn't big enough to accommodate them. Glancing back toward the advancing swarm, he looked back to the inner gate and locked eyes with the guard stood above it.

Boring every ounce of his authority into the tall blonde man, he shouted the single command which could save them all.

It would save the town, but it would condemn every man, woman, child, and animal left in the new part of the town. Maybe a hundred people would have to pay the ultimate needed to save the whole of Three Hills.

Drawing in his breath, his brain reminding him that this was his last chance to find another solution, he bawled the order.

"Cut it!"

The tall blonde man swallowed, hefted the blade in his right hand, and chopped down on the rope holding the gate up to make the heavy wood slam down and seal the gap.

The screams from below, Harrison knew, would stay with him for his entire life.

Epilogue

Harrison walked along the burned, blackened ramparts that had survived the spreading flames. All night the occupants of the walled town had passed bags and buckets of water from their supply hand over hand until the last of the fires had been extinguished.

Those who had been trapped below, locked out of the safety they all enjoyed inside an un-breached wall, screamed incessantly until their screams were stopped either by the swarming insects the size of cats or by the choking fumes of the fires.

Now that the fire and Swarm ravaged area could be accessed, Harrison donned his vest and long knives and led a party of warriors in to seal the hole in the wall and search for survivors.

There were none.

Using his foot to break down a damaged wooden door to one of the single-story buildings, the scene before him broke his heart and threatened to rob him of the ability to walk.

The bright white bones arrayed before him told a tale of love and desperation. Of bravery and utter acceptance of a terrible fate. A skeleton had the long bones of its arms wrapped around a pile of smaller bones, all picked as clean as the others he had seen. Leaning forward, his body froze as his eyes locked on to the two small rounded shapes in that pile, and the presence of the tiny skulls made him imagine a scene that he would never forget.

A mother, or a father as the skeleton would not tell him which, had covered their children as The Swarm broke in and devoured them where they lay. He imagined the crying as the screeching, roiling mass of bugs splintered their way through the flimsy barricade, then the screams of agony as the first bites were taken from their bodies and the rapid absence of human sounds as they died and were consumed.

But Harrison did not cry. He did not break down and scream and curse anyone. He did not vomit and fall into a catatonic state, but instead he closed the door on the heartbreaking family scene and organized the repairs to the wall to be made and for graves to be dug.

He had work to do, and there was no time for sentiment.

About the Author

Devon C Ford is from the UK and lives in the Midlands. His career in public services started in his teens and has provided a wealth of experiences, both good and some very bad, which form the basis of the books ideas that cause regular insomnia.

Facebook: @decvoncfordofficial

Twitter: @DevonFordAuthor

Website: www.devoncford.com

The *After it Happened* series

Set in the UK in the immediate aftermath of a mysterious illness which swept the country and left millions dead, the series follows the trials facing a reluctant hero, Dan, and the group that forms around him.

www.vulpine-press.com/after-it-happened

The Fall

Cal's 'honeymoon' didn't start off quite how he'd planned. For starters, he was heading somewhere he didn't actually want to go. And secondly, he was going alone and unmarried. He had no idea that his first visit to New York City would also land him in the middle of a domestic terror attack, forcing him to flee Manhattan in a desperate bid to survive.

www.vulpine-press.com/burning-skies

32139454R00155

Printed in Great Britain
by Amazon